*Praise for One Little Lie*

'A big tangled mess of lies that I couldn't put
down … Wild and brilliantly written, I loved it'

VOGUE WILLIAMS

'A must for your book club. Provocative,
emotionally challenging and everyone
will have an opinion - guaranteed'

IMOGEN CLARK

'Despicable, controversial and
peep-through-your-fingers compelling.
A marmite must-read for book clubs'

RACHEL SARGEANT

'This beautifully written story about how
one impulsive lie can spiral into catastrophic
consequences will stay with me for a long time.
Does one bad choice really make you a bad person?'

LOUISE JENSEN

'[*One Little Lie*] is so well researched and plays
with the dark and light of lies and trust in a way
that made me try to understand Sarah's behaviour,
veering from sympathy to disgust. Fabulous read'

JACQUELINE WARD

'Dark, original, thought-provoking
and utterly compelling'

LOUISE BEECH

'An intense read with a plot that spirals towards disaster, *One Little Lie* is deeply provocative, often painful, and sure to get conversations flowing. I couldn't look away even when I was screaming in frustration at each dangerous choice that Sarah, the central character, made'

LUCY ASHE

'*One Little Lie* ties together the urgent and mundane with expert precision. Just when you are lulled by the familiarity of a scene, you're hit with another jolt of the dark and unexpected. You won't want to put it down'

GEMMA HARTLEY

'A taut, emotional read guaranteed to provoke heated debate about what women do, and do not want from domestic life and marriage. This thought-provoking book asks questions about gender roles and where responsibility lies. I raced through it, and the questions it poses have stayed with me well beyond closing the final page'

CLOVER STROUD

'This novel articulates something many people feel but rarely say out loud: how easy it is to lose yourself in the care of everyone else. Provocative, powerful and impossible not to talk about afterwards'

CELIA SILVANI

# CHARLOTTE LEONARD

# One Little Lie

SIMON & SCHUSTER

London · New York · Amsterdam/Antwerp · Sydney/Melbourne · Toronto · New Delhi

First published in Great Britain by Simon & Schuster UK Ltd, 2026



1 3 5 7 9 10 8 6 4 2

Simon & Schuster UK Ltd, 7th Floor
199 Bishopsgate, London EC2M 3TY



Simon & Schuster Australia, Sydney
Simon & Schuster India, New Delhi

www.simonandschuster.co.uk
www.simonandschuster.com.au
www.simonandschuster.co.in

The authorised representative in the EEA is Simon & Schuster Netherlands BV, Herculesplein 96, 3584 AA Utrecht, Netherlands. info@simonandschuster.nl

Simon & Schuster strongly believes in freedom of expression and stands against censorship in all its forms. For more information, visit BooksBelong.com.

A CIP catalogue record for this book is available from the British Library

PB ISBN: 978-1-3985-0956-6
eBook ISBN: 978-1-3985-0955-9
Audio ISBN: 978-1-3985-1321-1



Typeset in Bembo by M Rules
Printed and Bound in the UK using 100% Renewable Electricity at CPI Group (UK) Ltd

To my family
Who can all leave a kitchen spotless
(And occasionally do)

# Prologue

*The house was hollow. Empty. Still. Devoid of all the people that I loved. I sat there in the gloom, the hall steeped in my memories. If I closed my eyes, I could see Ryan as a toddler in his favourite shorts, struggling to tie his shoelaces, and Olly banished to the naughty step, singing loudly with his head tipped back, his heels banging on the wooden floor, totally unfazed by it all. And James arriving home with flowers on Mother's Day, his arms filled with a bouquet of pink hyacinths, the blooms a mass of coloured stars.*

*Outside the sun was dying. A single piece of Sellotape came suddenly unstuck, pulling at a small patch of beige paintwork as it detached from the hallway wall. The 'Congratulations' banner collapsed until it was hanging by the final 's', the remainder of the letters twisting as they fell, and trailing down towards the wooden floor. It sounded like a moth hitting a lightbulb. The softest clunk. A sickening thud of singeing wings.*

*Inside the empty kitchen, a large bouquet of roses wrapped in* tissue and clear cellophane was propped inside a water jug, and left out on the clean table. Below the blooms of crimson petals was a spread of cards in brightly coloured envelopes, all with 'Mum' or 'Sarah' written on the front, in handwriting that I recognised. I edged a nail into a gap and forced the gummed paper apart to rip open the card from James. 'You've always been a star to me and both our boys,' James had written in his familiar scrawl.

The words felt like a stomach punch. I pulled one hand towards my heart, pressed the other hand firmly on top, as if trying to staunch a fatal bleed. An injury no one could see. My heart pounded at frantic speed, as I ripped open the remaining cards.

'I love you, Mum.'

'We all love you.'

I sank into a chair and placed my head flat on the table, felt the sparkling clean and bleached surface press up against my pounding skull. I closed my eyes.

'I love you too,' I said out loud to all of them.

But there was no one there to hear me.

# PART ONE

# The Two-Week Wait

James left me in the morning with a pile of dirty washing and a kiss. The kiss was a hardly a kiss at all. No press of lips. No eyes that sparked. Instead, he pecked me on the forehead as if I were a child.

It hadn't always been like this. In the years after the boys were born, I would wait inside the open door and watch my husband cross the street as he walked away in the direction of the tube and his office somewhere in the city. I can still conjure his disappearing form, his thick dark hair, razored to form a straight and steady line in the soft hollow where neck meets skull. My own dependable horizon. At the corner he would pause and turn and wave goodbye and I would wave goodbye and press my hands over the ribs that housed my heart and later he would call me just to tell me that he missed me. But that was years and years before. His hair was now streaked concrete grey, not glossy black, and instead of waving in the mornings he would leave me in the kitchen with a heap of dirty laundry and a kiss. A kiss that honestly did not deserve its name.

I glanced around the kitchen at the chaos. Strewn along the worktop above the open dishwasher there were random plates and dirty bowls. Glasses nursed abandoned drinks and hardened crusts from late-night snacks were spread across the cutting board beside an open pack of butter, the golden shape collapsing in the morning warmth. A solitary coffee cup had been forgotten by the kettle, its sides smeared with pink lip gloss, and I wondered why I'd ever let my eldest son move his girlfriend Bo into his bedroom.

Picking up the coffee cup I sighed and began to load the empty dishwasher. I wanted to make breakfast, but the pile of dirty laundry was distracting. I tried to pretend that the shirts didn't exist, but every time I went to walk across the room my toes got caught on empty sleeves, absent limbs clutching at mine. I kicked the pile, kicked it hard until the clothes were all shoved up against the wall and out my way.

To this day I'm not exactly sure how it all happened. How I woke up with a man who hardly spoke to me and more children than I gave birth to, all grown up but still living inside a house that felt too small. That had never been the plan. It wasn't what I'd signed up for. It wasn't what I'd dreamed of.

If I try to imagine all of the things I would have wanted

then, I can't conjure what I might have said. Would I have asked for some new bath salts or a novel that I wouldn't find the time to read, or those delicious little chocolates wrapped in twists of shiny paper? But none of that stuff matters now because the thing that I most hoped for was for life to monumentally change, and in the end, I got exactly that. A different life. A massive change.

What a stupid, stupid thing for me to wish for.

Kicking the front door closed behind me, I paused. The house was still and quiet, hushed. Perhaps another premonition of the future I'd create shortly. But I had no idea in that moment of what was to come, and so the silence felt like some great gift. A shard of peace amongst the usual noisy chaos of my life. It was the day before my birthday and I remember that it felt joyful, the absence of sound. No bickering or loud music, no running showers or shouting or the constant slamming of the fridge. No annoying drone of TikTok reels on repeat. I was overjoyed. And so naïve. The things that I would give right now just to have a full and noisy house, to have a fraction of that chaos back. Being all alone is only joyful when you're not lonely. I know that now.

I sat down in the cool hallway, eased my sandals off, kneaded firmly at the fallen arches of my feet and loudly exhaled. My family would be back soon which made that rare moment of calm feel like something truly precious. Pacing the house, the unfamiliar oddity of unfilled time was almost stultifying as I moved from messy room to messy room.

I fought the urge to start cleaning and finally settled on a bath. It was just hours from my birthday, and I felt like I deserved it. The tap squeaked, and the water spat, then gushed, filling the tiny room up with a reassuring, gentle roar. Sitting on the bath edge, my generous thighs spread out over the narrow lip, my feet on the bald bathmat which was emitting the slight funk of constant damp. As I waited for the cold water to eventually run hot, I moved to absently pick clothes up off the floor and from around the empty wash basket; discarded pants, inverted socks, and T-shirts turned inside out. I still found it amazing that the boys I'd raised could shoot a basketball into a hoop from miles away but couldn't drop some dirty clothes into a large container placed directly at their feet.

Unpeeling my own clothes, my hand brushed something solid, something strange. For a second, I wasn't entirely sure what I had felt. My heart faltered. My breath grew barbed and caught somewhere inside my lungs. I must have looked ridiculous, my blouse stuck halfway over my head, like a cat recovering from surgery trying to escape the awkward plastic cone. I wrestled with the shirt buttons and tried to recollect exactly how to breathe. How a person made their lungs expand and then contract, repeatedly. Naked, standing on the damp bathmat, I pressed the pads of my fingers against my drooping breast. And there it was. A lump. The size of a small frozen pea embedded deep beneath the skin. Solid, smooth, and hard.

'It's just a lump, a normal lump. Women find lumps all the time,' I told myself, my heartbeat racing. Frenzied. Fast. 'It's probably absolutely nothing,' I repeated in a panicked mantra. But I couldn't help thinking about my mum, about the cancer cells that started in her ovaries, cells that crept and spread and crept and spread, until she was more cancer than my mother.

*Oh God*, I thought, whilst staring in the clouded bathroom mirror. *What if this is finally it? The beginning of the end for me.*

And my fears were right. It really was.

Although it wasn't quite the ending I'd imagined.

I pretended that the lump didn't exist, at least for the duration of my birthday. I hoped that it would go away. Some things are better off ignored, I told myself. But the lump's presence was quietly haunting. Arriving at the Day Centre for work I was greeted with a huge arch of balloons tied up with parcel string and a fat hand-painted 'Happy Birthday Sarah!' sign, the brushstrokes broad and clumsy.

'Surprise!' my colleagues cried, as I walked into the dining room, heading towards the staff room with my handbag tucked beneath one arm.

I stopped. Stood still.

Everyone I worked with, as well as all the older people who attended on a Wednesday, wore brightly coloured party hats; tight wraps of sugar paper stuck with lumpy smears of Pritt stick, like little upside-down Cornetto cones. On a table, there was a slightly slanted birthday cake, a vanilla sponge piled high with juicy strawberries and, beside it, a stack of birthday cards.

I remember feeling overwhelmed. I pressed my hand across my chest as the whole room sang. Casey fumbled with a lighter, then walked the cake towards me with her arms outstretched. She winked as she grew close. The strawberries smelled of the bathroom after Bo showered. I watched the candles flickering as I waited for the song to end and tried my hardest not to think about my evening. James would likely be home late again. Ryan would be playing on his PlayStation, smoking weed out of his window, and Bo and Olly would have commandeered the living room. My evening would be just the same as all my other evenings.

After the clapping and the cheering and the sharing of the cake out onto flimsy paper plates, I went to sit with Donna at the craft table. Donna was my favourite, although I tried my hardest not to let the others know. At eighty-nine she still loved clothes, ensuring that her outfits always matched and that the colours of her many different cardigans co-ordinated with the jewellery she wore. That day the string of beads around her neck were cornflower blue, the individual beads like eggs, her skirt a deep, rich navy. She squeezed my hand, then reached into the basket of her walker, pushing a card across the table past the little piles of mosaic tiles and plastic pots of pre-mixed grout.

'Happy Birthday, Sarah,' she said, smiling.

The writing on the envelope was as thin as thread, the lines precarious and rickety. Inside the card she'd written in her jolting hand, 'Thank you for absolutely everything you do. You make my weekdays joyful. It's hard to find the words to tell you just how wonderful you are.' I rubbed the thin skin of my eyelids.

'You're much too kind,' I said, shaking my head and collecting up the cool flesh of her bone-spurred hand.

'It's not kindness. It's just the truth,' she said briskly. 'I believe that we should tell things as they truly are.' She placed a hand on top of mine, giving it a gentle pat.

At the time I didn't really hear her words, didn't realise they were words that I should take note of, should live by. After all, our truths are all we have. All that any of us really have.

I left work late that evening and walked towards the bus stop. As the light began to quickly fade, the colours became flat and dull. Above my head a cloud had formed, a thunderstorm, a darkness, and my sweat-drenched clothes were cooling faster than the air. I shuddered and took out my phone.

'How's the birthday going?' Nel asked me, her voice upbeat.

But I couldn't think of any words.

'Nel?' I said instead, the word wobbling.

My voice sounded too distant, far away, as if it wasn't really mine. It was hard to hear myself these days, over the new-found fear which made a constant fizzing sound inside my head, like the static from a radio.

'What's wrong? Are you okay?' Nel asked.

Across the road, a woman gripped a toddler's hand. He was writhing, trying to free himself. He veered towards the traffic as she held on tight.

'I'm not sure what to do,' I said, as the woman yanked the child back, away from all the speeding cars.

There was a pause as I attempted to put my worry into words. Tightness was building in my throat and when I spoke again my voice was strained, the sound muffled and strangled.

'I've found something,' I finally said, 'I'm not sure what I'm meant to do.'

And then, I told my oldest friend.

I'd found a lump.

~

The next morning, I woke before the others and crept as quietly as possible downstairs. I poured myself a glass of water at the cluttered sink. The night before, my family had all told me that because it was my birthday, I didn't need to touch a thing, but they hadn't touched things either. There were bowls clotted with Coco Pops, an abandoned empty milk carton and numerous plates piled into a tower, the food they'd failed to scrape into the bin squashed between ceramic layers. I shivered in the morning air. My pyjamas still felt damp, the remnants of hormonal sweats, and I smelled strongly of vinegar and yeast. A perfect storm of morning mess and frazzled mind.

I probably should have left things as they were but the thought of coming home to even more domestic chaos was almost overwhelming. It was easier to do the thing I usually did and just clean up, so I started off another day fishing dishes out of the cold water, my skin wrinkling and creasing in the tepid greasy scum. The washing conjured silent rage, which grew with every dish I cleaned, until I found that I was slamming drawers and clinking plates, loudly banging all the cupboards closed. It didn't seem too much to want my family to acknowledge all the work I did and to occasionally say thank you, but despite the noise no one appeared.

I got to work at least an hour early and headed to the only quiet café, the one beside the zebra crossing with the temperamental traffic lights. The place served mediocre coffee from an old machine, and it smelled of bitter beans; the coffee always singed. I sat down at a table with a cup of acrid decaf and a muffin stained with blueberries. The walls were painted deep maroon and displayed a breadth of pictures, badly framed, the work of local artists on rotation. The pictures when I visited that day were watercolour paintings of nearby landmarks (the gold-domed mosque, the post office, the 1920s cinema with its charismatic blocky font) and local houses when the trees that lined the streets were thick with spring blossom. The prices made me laugh out loud, each picture costing more than my week's wages, and I recall thinking that I could have done a better job, if only I'd had time.

I'd promised Nel I'd ring first thing to make an appointment with a doctor and after a night crammed full of nightmares of my dying mum, I couldn't put off calling any longer. I dialled the number eleven times before I made the telephone queue and was put on hold in seventh place. The receptionist finally answered, her voice thick with disinterest.

'Face-to-face or telephone?' she barked. 'And what exactly is the problem?'

I'm pretty sure I stuttered, struggling with the words to tell her of the terrifying thing I'd found but when I did her tone changed.

'Can you come today?' she asked, the potential seriousness of the situation granting me rare access to an appointment that same day. Her kindness was unusual and if I'm honest I quite liked it. The attention. The sincere concern.

'I have to go to work right now,' I stammered, fiddling with the grease-stained empty muffin case, but she told me that they had some later slots on hold, especially for emergencies like this and asked if I could get to her by six.

The details of the doctor's appointment are a chaotic mix of blurry mess and pin-prick sharp. I can't remember what the room was like, or what the duty doctor wore. But I can still recall her mousy face and mousy hair and the fact she didn't look much older than my sons. I remember wondering about her home, if she rode a bicycle to work or travelled by tube, if she had a partner or a pet or suffered from bad allergies. Her desk was neat and organised, and I suspected that she threw all the spices out her cupboards and the condiments from out her fridge before they'd passed their use-by date. It's strange, the details that you fixate on when your mind is grim with worry.

I've never felt as naked as I did whilst sitting in that room with my trousers on, top and bra discarded on a chair. I shivered from the cold or was it simply that I felt exposed? Too vulnerable. Too human with my breasts on show.

The young doctor requested that I press my hands onto

my hips and that I hold out my arms like chicken wings. I felt ridiculous, but I did exactly what she asked and when I looked down at my sagging breasts, I saw the marks that stretched like silvered lightning strikes or the feathered frost that creeps across my window on cold mornings in the winter.

'Hmmm,' she said, her face furrowed in concentration as she felt. 'Well, you're right, there is a lump right here, although the edges are distinct and well defined, which gives me less cause for concern than a lump with jagged edges.' I knew the words were meant to reassure me, but the doctor frowned as she was speaking and the knot inside my stomach failed to loosen. 'I've also read your notes, and given that you have a family history . . .' Her speech tapered to silence as she carried on pressing my chest, palpating the small lump with the cold pads of her fingertips. I shivered, goosebumps rising. 'I think it would be best if we refer you to the hospital. That way we'll know exactly what we're dealing with.' She gestured at my pile of clothes, indicating that I should get dressed, and began to briskly rearrange a pile of tidy papers on her desk, before she started typing. 'So, I've made you a referral on the urgent two-week pathway,' she said, still staring at her computer monitor. 'You'll hear directly from the hospital, and in the meantime try not to lose sleep. In my experience, these things are often nothing of significance.'

The doctor looked so young right then that I couldn't help but wonder just how much experience she really had. Her words lacked reassurance as I watched her face. I knew instinctively that she was wrong. The lump was of significance and it had the power to change my life in striking, monumental ways.

When I finally made it home, I found Nel waiting on the doorstep holding a bottle of red wine. The evening light was sultry pink as the sun began to sink behind the row of terraced houses.

'It's for me,' she said, following my gaze.

'Aren't you supposed to bring something for me? And you do know that we have wine here?'

'Well, you hardly ever drink, and I don't particularly trust Plank's judgement when it comes to buying wine.'

Plank was the name she'd given James almost thirty years ago when I first met him in a London bar. Nel used to joke that despite his handsome looks, his maths degree and solid job as an accountant, when it came to anything emotional, he acted like a plank of wood. 'Plenty more plank-ton in the sea,' she'd say and despite myself, I'd start to laugh. In retrospect, I think that she was nervous, not wanting any man to infiltrate our friendship and to change the way things were between the two of us. Nel and I had been inseparable since starting secondary school, and we'd attended the same art college. No one knew me better than she did. But nothing ever stays the same, and besides, back then, I loved him more than anything. Even more than Nel.

She pressed a lipsticked kiss into my cheek and then shimmied herself past me. Her perfume lingered in the hall as she headed to the kitchen. She smelled of cloves and firewood, of whisky and patchouli. As I closed the door, I raised a hand to wave hello to a neighbour who was dragging her recycling out, wrestling with the giant bin. The bin's wheels kept catching on uneven paving slabs and the woman didn't notice me.

'He's not *that* bad,' I said, shutting the door and turning to Nel.

She looked unconvinced.

Nel began to rummage through a kitchen drawer with her gouache-splattered fingers, digging her way through salad spoons and sausage tongs, all the knives that needed sharpening and a random meat thermometer that James had gifted me one Christmas.

Eventually she found a corkscrew and stabbed at the cork. She gripped the bottle with her knees and wrestled the wine open with a grunt of satisfaction.

'What do you mean, "He's not that bad"?' she said. 'Are we referring to your husband's taste when it comes to choosing wine or simply to your husband?' She crinkled up her small, neat nose and began searching for a wine glass. Or any glass at all that appeared clean. She flung another cupboard door open and peered.

'I know,' I said, my voice forlorn. 'It was tidy when I left for work. I genuinely don't know how they create this amount of mess. If it wasn't me who had to clean it up, I'd almost be impressed.'

Nel scanned the room, looked unimpressed. 'Where are they all?'

'Out,' I said. 'Well, all except for Ryan who will be upstairs and plugged into his PC with the curtains closed and headphones on.'

'Probably watching porn,' said Nel.

I shut my eyes against the thought. When I opened them again, she was swigging a large mouthful of red wine. 'So,' she said. She placed the wine down on the table and gave me a long look. 'Are you feeling any better?'

I shrugged.

'But the doctor said the lump was smooth, and smooth lumps are usually fine?'

'Apparently,' I said, fiddling with a piece of thread that was unravelling from my T-shirt.

I tried my hardest to sound nonchalant, but I was genuinely anxious. In fact, I felt far worse now that the presence of the lump had been confirmed by someone else. It no longer existed within the confines of my own dark fears. I'd also started googling, finding random stories of smooth, soft lumps that had turned out to be cancerous. I was certain that my lump was cancerous too.

'Umm, what the hell is that?' I asked, changing the subject, pointing at a giant blue Ikea bag that Nel had abandoned by the table.

'Some sketchbooks that I need to mark.' She pulled a random book from the bag and flipped open the pages. 'Just look at this. It's by a student in year ten, a self-portrait. I'm trying to give some feedback that's constructive, but there isn't all that much to say.'

'Is that supposed to be an actual face?' I asked, sounding incredulous.

Nel turned her neck as if the painting would improve somehow if viewed from a new angle.

'Were they in some awful accident that involved a vat of acid?'

We couldn't help but laugh.

'No, he's just not any good at art.' She picked the sketchbook up and turned the whole thing round. 'Although he does have cystic acne, so . . .'

Nel's laughter made her head move and the evening light got tangled in the glitter flecks embedded in her eyeshadow.

'I really don't know how you teach,' I said.

'And I have absolutely no idea how you spend your days caring for those old people! When I visit Mum's dementia home, they all smell a bit like cabbage, don't you think?'

'Of course they don't!'

Nel pulled a face of disbelief, and I couldn't help but think about the faint smell of ammonia that always seemed to hang around the Day Centre, loitering, unwanted, ever-present, like the school kids at the corner shop.

'Anyway, I bought this for your birthday,' she said, placing a plait-end in her mouth and chewing on the tendrils so that I could hear the crunch of gnawing hair.

Nel rummaged in her bag again until she found what she was looking for. A package wrapped in matt paper, the orange of a traffic cone and dotted with hand-painted stars.

'Thanks, Nel,' I said. I unwrapped the parcel slowly, peeled the paper like an onion. Inside there was a new sketchbook with crisp pages and a cover made of leather with my maiden name embossed along the solid spine.

'Do you know something I don't?' I asked, my eyebrows raised as I stroked the cursive letters of my former name. And then I beamed at her. 'I really, really love it, Nel.'

'There's more,' she said. Beneath the empty drawing book there was a tin filled with new pencils. I stroked them with my fingers, and the feeling was familiar, like returning to an instrument that I hadn't played in years. 'You really need to draw again. All that talent that you have, Sarah. All that time we spent at art college. I haven't seen you draw or paint since the boys were born, and you're too talented to just give up!'

'They're beautiful,' I said and then I glanced towards the laundry basket which was straining with the weight of dirty crumpled clothes, clean crumpled clothes that the boys had failed to put away and fitted sheets that even after all these years I couldn't fathom how to fold. I looked down at the tabletop and tapped one foot against the floor. 'I was waiting for the boys to both move out so that I'd have the space for my own studio again.' I paused. 'But I might have waited too long. What if there isn't time?'

'Oh, Sarah. You can stop that now!' She was coiling one damp plait around her finger. It looked just like the broadband cables that BT were laying in the road.

'But what if . . . ?'

'Don't think that way. I'm sure it's absolutely nothing, like the doctor said, but even if it is cancer, a single course of chemo might be all it takes.'

She made it sound so easy. Just 'a single course of chemo'. But I thought back to the horror of my mum's treatment. The radiation and the chemicals that made the jelly ache inside her bones. Huge quantities of steroids that kept her moving through the sluggish days and wide-awake and wired throughout the awful, elongated nights. I was worried that I'd found the lump too late, that it was cancerous and spreading to my organs at a frightening rate. I spiralled into torment and catastrophe.

'It's going to be alright, Sarah,' Nel said.

'What if it's not?' I said, my voice shrinking. 'Ryan is incapable of making his own bed, although I'm not sure if that matters much. I mean, he hardly leaves his room. And Olly and Bo can only cook things out of packages that have instructions printed on the back. I've failed as a mother, Nel. They'll all develop scurvy if I die.'

I may have sounded overly dramatic.

'You're not dying.'

'You don't know that.'

'Neither do you! And anyway, you're not the only parent here. If you need to go through treatment, then the boys have Plank.'

There was silence for a second as we caught each other's eyes, and the corners of our lips began to creep towards our cheeks.

When Dad had died and I'd gone to sort the contents of his house, the boys survived off buttered toast and bowls of Kellogg's Rice Krispies. The meals kindly cooked by Nel were relegated to the bin. She had made the big mistake of cooking foods that weren't entirely beige, that contained some actual vegetables and a vast array of spices. Left alone with James and Nel, the boys would struggle to survive.

'It will be fine,' Nel reassured. 'I'll buy them multivitamins.'

'No vodka then?' I asked, my eyebrows raised.

'Alright. Okay. I learned my lesson last time. But in my defence, I thought that teenage boys would be much better with their booze.'

'Ryan was only just fifteen!'

'Exactly. Our entire generation was great at drinking by fifteen.'

I shook my head, remembering the stories that we'd told, claiming to be at sleepovers, at the cinema or in Café Rouge when the truth was we were in the pub.

'And anyway, he's older now. And the boys can mix their vodka with fresh orange juice which will help fight off the scurvy.' Nel generously refilled her glass and fiddled with the label on the wine bottle. 'So, have you told him yet? What did he say?'

I shook my head. 'Not yet.'

'Sarah!' she reprimanded. 'I know that he's emotionally incompetent but isn't sharing what a marriage is supposed to be about?'

The judgement stung. I said nothing.

'Why wouldn't you just tell him?'

'I'm not quite sure,' I said finally.

But of course I knew. After decades married to my husband, I could predict the ways he would respond. He would either say too little, hoping that the problem might just go away all by itself. Or conversely, he would say too much and bombard me with statistics, attempt to minimise my feelings. And then there was the bigger issue. The thing that truly haunted me.

'I'm not sure that he loves me, Nel.'

The room swelled with the gushing of the dishwasher.

'Of course he does!' Nel said loudly. She stopped ripping thin paper strips from off the wine label. I watched her fingers interlace.

'I'm really not convinced he does. Not anymore,' I quietly said.

'Sarah . . .' She shook her head.

'James just sees me as another adult living in the house. One that does all of the cooking and the cleaning. I mean, we don't have sex. We never talk. It's just so sad.'

Nel's body visibly convulsed at the mention of sex with James, and she took a hefty swig of wine, swirled it around her mouth. Then she reached and took my hand tightly in hers. I could feel the dents and ridges of her heavy silver rings.

'I just don't know,' I said. 'I always thought that when the boys grew up, James and I could focus on our marriage. Maybe go away on holiday, find a new way for the two of us. But it's all just wishful thinking. I think that it might be too late.'

'Of course it's not,' Nel said, but I wasn't really listening.

'Ryan won't manage to ever get a job. He'll just live with us forever, and Bo and Olly will still be here too. They'll never save enough to buy a flat. And now I might be really sick, James will see me as a burden. Something broken.'

Nel took a breath and squeezed my hand a little harder.

'I know that things aren't perfect but perhaps you're just projecting. Are you sure that *you* still love him?'

I pulled my hand away and rubbed the furrows that her rings had left. I focused on a large indent, where a piece of mounted rose quartz had pressed into my ring finger.

I thought about the love that authors write about in novels and that we get to see in movies. A wild and crazy, intense love with lightning strikes, bright fireworks and neon hearts. I'd felt that way when James and I were first together. I had loved him so intensely that it physically hurt. I would look at him and lose my breath and every time he kissed me, I would lose myself. But now it seemed that we merely co-existed, bound together by our shared offspring, a joint mortgage and household bills. I still loved him, but something had been lost over the years. I wanted what we used to have and there was nothing, absolutely nothing, that I wouldn't do or wouldn't give to have it back.

It was dark when James came home later.

Nel had left an hour earlier, and I'd been sitting on the sofa for the first time in what felt like weeks. I heard James grab the banister and swear beneath his too-loud breath as he removed his shiny leather shoes. He padded into the living room with heavy feet and sank down on the smaller sofa, the one the cat had commandeered as its own personal scratch post.

James flopped his head backwards so it rested on the sofa back and stretched his toes inside his socks.

'How was your day?' I tried.

'Long,' he said, eyes closed. I turned my face towards the window and saw the couple opposite who were always writing on the neighbourhood WhatsApp group to complain about their misplaced bins and the council's latest plans to introduce controlled parking.

'Is there anything for dinner, love?' James eventually asked.

I pursed my lips. 'You said you'd be home late tonight. I thought you'd eat at work.'

His nostrils made a whistling sound as he let out a slow exhale. His greying hair was looking long, in desperate need of cutting. The furrows on his forehead had become so deep that even with his face relaxed his skin was creased. There were faint grey smudges beneath his eyes that make him look like Bo did in the morning when she'd drunk too much the night before and had slept wearing mascara.

'There's lasagne left over in the fridge,' I said.

James didn't move.

'I could microwave it for you?'

'Please,' James said, opening his eyes.

As I pulled myself to standing, I cupped one hand around my breast. Subconsciously. Instinctively. I pressed my fingers flat into the flesh and felt it there. I felt the lump. I briefly paused.

'Are you okay?' he asked, his eyes narrowed, and I wondered if he knew right then, suspected something wasn't right or could hear what I was thinking. The secret quietly deafening.

'I'm fine,' I said, pulling my hand away, stepping back into the hallway. I could hear keys jangling in the lock and Bo and Olly laughing hard as they wrestled the Chubb open. Then, there they were — standing on the scuffed door mat. It was dark outside, suburban dark, which wasn't all that dark at all but a murky, muddied dull expanse littered with the lights of planes that moved like travelling man-made stars. The fact the streetlight didn't work (an issue that the members of the WhatsApp group often discussed) had only made it slightly darker. Framed against the muted backdrop of the London night, I could only see one silhouette. The shape two people make when they let down all their borders. My heart contracted tightly. I wanted that. I really did. To be that close to James again. And for him to want to be that close to me.

The following evening there was no one on the doorstep when I made it home. Ryan had called an hour earlier, to tell me he was locked outside and that he couldn't find his housekeys. I'd arranged to leave work early, leaving Casey with too much to do, and had jogged to catch the crowded bus. Now, I clearly wasn't needed. From the narrow hallway, I could hear raised voices from the kitchen. It seemed that everyone was home and fighting over what to do for food. Bo was arguing against pizza, telling all the others that she'd gone off carbs, at least until her girls' weekend in Brighton.

'Then what about Szechuan Delight? They make a really good chow mein.' I heard James reply.

'Sounds great,' said Bo.

'You know that noodles count as carbs,' Ryan attempted to explain.

'Oh, I think I've got my carbs confused with gluten. I'll just have a large chicken chow mein.'

'Chow mein and pizza both contain . . .'

Olly quickly interrupted, telling Ryan he should shut his face. 'Or we won't be getting any dinner at this rate.'

I shook my head as I hung my leather handbag on the bottom wooden banister and threw my sandals somewhere in the darkness of the shoe cupboard. Olly's trainers lay abandoned on the hallway floor, and I picked them up by the long laces. The trainers smelled of vinegar, hard-boiled eggs and Original Doritos. My stomach churned as I flung them in the cupboard with the other shoes and slammed the door. My face was now fully on fire. I walked into the kitchen where my family and Bo were sat around the table scrolling through menus on separate phones. I could hear hot blood throb in my ears.

'Are you kidding me?'

Everybody stopped and turned to stare, and I watched their faces flush before they looked away, as if I'd caught them doing something truly awful. It reminded me of the time that Olly left the bathroom door unlocked, and I found him with my pink razor, manscaping all his newly sprouted pubes. 'So, you made it inside the house I see,' I said, glaring at Ryan. 'And there's food right here. There's tonnes of food. I went to Tesco only yesterday. The fridge is full, and I made a chicken casserole!'

'We're too tired to cook,' said James, attempting to explain, 'and we didn't know where you had gone. Did you know Ryan was stuck outside? It's a good job that I came home when I did.'

I was momentarily lost for words, until the anger flooded thick and fast. 'The casserole is sitting there! Surely one of you could heat it up? And I get tired too, but I still cook!'

Bo was staring at her painted nails. She began to rub the polish firmly with her thumb, as if the smudging action might erase the neon shade. Yet again I wondered why I'd let her stay here while she and Olly saved up for a flat. She was a temporary addition who now seemed permanent.

'But you're really good at cooking, Sarah. I mean, you've had a lot of practice.'

I swung around. 'Oh, fuck off, Bo!'

The air became frighteningly still. The only sound was the cat slurping at a meaty pile of wet cat food.

'Mum!' Olly shouted. His face had turned a purple shade. 'You can't speak to Bo like that.'

Even Ryan looked perturbed. His jaw hung slack and his eyes widened.

'I've spent hours cooking for you lot. If you add it up its probably years. You ungrateful bunch of . . .'

James quickly interrupted then and suggested that I go lie down.

'We'll order you a bowl of Szechuan noodles,' he tentatively tried. James looked confused, as if the rules of how our family worked had suddenly changed, and he had failed to get the memo.

'Oh, screw you and your noodles too. You're always going on about the fact that we don't have money spare to waste on things as frivolous as takeaways.'

I slammed the kitchen door shut, rattling the frame, then opened it again before grabbing the saucepan from the stove. I threw the lid into the sink and emptied all the cold congealed casserole into the bin. A dribble of brown liquid trailed down the outside of the metal bin leaving a mess that I would have to clean up later. My family watched in silence as I slammed the kitchen door shut for a second time.

As I stomped upstairs, I heard them whispering amongst themselves, but I only caught a single word. Apparently, I was going through the menopause.

*Menopause.*

The final straw. That muttered word. The thing that broke the camel's back.

What followed next was a sort of mini mental breakdown. I'm not quite sure how else I can explain it. All I know is that I went to bed. And stayed in bed. I wouldn't move. The bed was now an island in a domestic, dusty sea. I could hear James's lumbering large footsteps as he climbed the stairs and then walked towards our bedroom. I shut my eyes as he waited in the doorway. The cat had clearly followed James, and I felt it jump onto the bed and begin to paddle with its paws, pushing on the bedding just above my knees, its claws fully extended.

'Sarah, this has got to stop.' James's voice was quiet and urgent. 'Aren't you getting up today?' he asked. I stayed exactly where I was and actively ignored him. 'Also, no one put the bins out for collection, so they didn't get emptied this week. I'm not sure what I'm meant to do. The green recycling one is full.' More minutes passed. 'Can't you go and ask the doctor for some HRT?'

I rolled over and groaned into the safety of the pillow-case, pulled the duvet higher above my head. None of this had been the plan. I still had dreams. I needed time. Now my body was probably rotting from the inside out, like cellophane-wrapped supermarket meat that had passed its expiration date and was emitting a revolting smell, something fetid, foul and almost sweet, whilst my family blamed my hormones.

'Sarah?' James was pleading now. 'This makes no sense.'

I didn't move. I didn't speak. He cleared his throat.

'You'll be okay,' James carried on. His voice was sounding desperate now and his words lacked reassurance. 'It's just the hormones talking, love. Or maybe it's the lack of them? I'm not quite sure how these things work.'

The silence hung between us, as I failed to answer yet again. I stayed corpse still and didn't move until James finally walked away.

'Oh God, woman. What's going on? Please don't tell me that you've been seen at the hospital already? Oh Sarah. No! You should have said. Is it bad news?'

I must have been asleep when she came in. I recognised the voice of Nel and could smell strong perfume in the air. It reminded me of fresh pineapples, of wood polish and every single long-fringed boy that I fancied in the 90s.

'Not yet. The appointment is next week,' I sighed into

the pillow, with its pale stains of air-dried drool. 'Are you wearing CK One?' I asked, after a pause.

I pushed the duvet down an inch so that my eyes appeared and I blinked against the brilliance of daylight. Nel was wearing a loose kaftan that looked as if a local-council flowerbed had been attacked with a machete and flung onto the fabric.

'I am!' she said, looking quite pleased. 'It's made a massive comeback. Have you noticed Bo and both your sons? They might as well have stolen all their outfits from our teen wardrobes. Did you know that MC Hammer is on tour again?' The scent evoked strong memories. Of fervent kisses, clashing teeth and the simple joys of dry humping in denim jeans. I remembered feeling so alive, the future spread ahead of me, exciting and unwritten still. Now I faced only an ending, an untimely death. I'd decided that I might as well remain in bed.

'I'll make us both a cup of tea while you go and have a shower,' Nel said. 'We could drink it in the garden.'

'I don't want to wash. I'm staying here.'

Nel shook her head and her purple beaded earrings swung. She was picking random bottles up from off my chest of drawers and squinting at the labels. There were little tubs and tiny tubes all filled with sticky serums, opaque creams and a range of creamy lotions that claimed they could do magic things; hydrate, rejuvenate, renew. I wondered why it is was that I kept buying them when they failed so spectacularly to turn back time.

'I really love you, Sarah, but this room smells worse than Ryan's does.'

I ignored this.

'Did James call you?' I asked instead.

'Yes,' she said, putting down a tub of hand cream. 'He was panicking about the bins. Then he mentioned you were still in bed. What's going on?'

Nel settled on the bedroom floor beside my head, her legs stretched out and her back against the old Ikea wardrobe that I'd put together by myself despite the fact the *Songesand* instructions clearly stated the construction was a two-man job.

'I can't get up,' I muttered.

'Is this all about the lump, Sarah?'

I nodded my head and lay there as a single tear escaped the corner of my eye.

'My family sucks. And I'm pretty sure I'm dying, Nel.'

Outside a pigeon loudly cooed. I clenched the duvet with a hand, clasped the fabric in a rigid fist.

'Oh, Sarah love. You're probably not.'

But as she spoke she came over and hugged me. She held onto me so tightly that I wondered if she thought that I would dissipate, evaporate into the air, leaving her alone embracing only emptiness. We stayed together on the bed, both hanging on.

'I'm going to be exactly like my mum,' I said. Or thought. I can't recall precisely which.

'Nope,' she finally said, pulling her body fully upright and dabbing at her eyes with the bottom of her kaftan. 'I love you, but you smell too bad. I don't care if you *are* dying – which I'm sure you're not! You're still getting in that shower.'

Despite my many protests, the fresh water felt insanely good. I washed my hair and body with a supermarket brand shampoo and then sprayed myself too liberally with something that turned out to be Olly's black Lynx Africa.

I found Nel sitting in the kitchen where she physically recoiled.

'I think you might have smelled better before you washed.' She walked towards me cautiously, her nose scrunched up, and handed me a cup of tea. 'You need to tell your family now, you really do. You need some more support and it's just not fair to keep them in the dark. It's time to tell the truth, Sarah.'

Nel was annoyingly persuasive and persistent. Apparently, it's not polite to hide away, thinking you're about to die without informing people first, particularly your loved ones. I quickly pointed out that I felt nothing close to love for Bo, and that since the menopause comment I had my reservations about James, but Nel chose to ignore me. She suggested that she stayed for dinner and that she did the talking for me.

'You don't have to,' I weakly said. 'They're *my* family.'

But then I looked around the kitchen. Clearly nobody had washed a thing since my 'small hormonal outburst'. The wash basket was spilling clothes over the floor and looked just like an animal the cat had dragged inside, fabric entrails overflowing everywhere. The sink was piled high with random bowls of cereal, Rice Krispie puffs glued to the sides like pale lumps of Polyfilla, and spread along the worktops there were grimy plates and mugs containing slops of tea and the grainy dregs of cold coffee.

'I can't sort this out,' I said, and I wondered if I meant the grim state of my kitchen or the situation with the lump. Hiding my face inside cupped hands, I realised I was crying. The tears leaked warm into my palms and caught inside the skin creases, ran like rivers down the hollows of what I then presumed were concerningly short lifelines.

'I'll help,' Nel said, her firm voice reassuring.

'But *you* can't clean this either. That's just not fair.'

Nel laughed out loud and told me she had absolutely no intention of cleaning up my family's dirty plates. 'They're all adults now,' she said, and I tried my very hardest to believe her.

'But what about dinner tonight? There isn't any space to cook.'

I gestured at the chaos that was once a kitchen worktop and began to cry more violently.

'I have a plan,' Nel finally said, as she jabbed intensely at her phone and so I let my oldest, dearest friend, send me back upstairs to bed. Allowing Nel to take control seemed like a genuine solution in the moment.

When everyone was home later that evening, I hid upstairs. Perching on the weathered steps, I picked at flecks of ginger fluff from where cat fur had merged into the carpet, until I had a tiny pile collected in my hand. I leaned closer to the banister and strained to glimpse into the kitchen. The only clear space was the table. Nel had pushed aside the breakfast plates, the lidless Lurpack tub, the two open pints of curdling milk. In the space that she'd created were five white sheets of toilet roll laid out in place of plates, and on each individual square of single ply, a sole digestive biscuit.

'Nel, what's going on?' James asked.

'Yeah? The text said there'd be dinner.' Olly pointed at the table, confusion disfiguring his youthful face, whilst Ryan sat nibbling at the edges of his biscuit.

'Is this gluten free?' Bo asked, prodding her biscuit. She frowned and chewed her dewy lip.

'This is all there is for dinner. And we need to talk,' Nel said.

'I'm not quite sure what's going on,' said James. He looked

unsettled as he picked up his toilet paper plate and the thin white sheet moved gently in the evening breeze that was coming from the open kitchen window.

Ryan brushed the biscuit crumbs from off his lap onto the floor. 'Are we going to get a lecture on the menopause?' Olly asked. 'Is that what's wrong with Mum right now?'

Nel ignored him. 'I have something to tell you all.'

I held my breath, but I couldn't stop myself from peering through the banister rails. Nel laid her hands palm down upon the table, her fingers splayed. She looked like someone lost in prayer. Or a judge about to hand a lengthy sentence out. Bo stopped picking at the polish on her fingernails and a deep silence descended.

I watched the colour disappear from Olly's face. 'Oh, God, she isn't pregnant? Please. That happened to a woman in our office. She thought that she was way too old but . . .' He turned towards his father, suddenly incensed. 'Dad! How could you be so stupid? You and mum are really ancient.'

'Stop!' said Nel. 'She's not pregnant.' There was a pause. 'We don't know what it is yet, and it could be absolutely nothing, but she's found a lump.'

For a fraction of a second, Olly almost looked relieved. 'So, there isn't a new baby?'

'No, there isn't a new baby. Your mother, well, she might be ill. And given that her mother died . . .'

More silence swamped the table until Bo began to cry.

Small sobs that made her breasts move rhythmically. Even crying, she looked beautiful.

Ryan slowly put his biscuit down.

'What kind of lump?' James whispered, his eyes the size of saucers. I clasped onto the banister.

'A breast lump, James. I'm sure that she'll be fine, but the GP has referred her to the hospital. The appointment is in seven days.'

'Oh God,' said James, his face ashen. He gripped onto the table edge. There was silence for a while save the usual London background sounds. A sharp siren. A distant hum. The droning of a lawnmower.

'Why is mum upstairs? Why isn't she down here?' Ryan suddenly asked, looking around.

'She's just a little overwhelmed right now. But seriously, do you blame her?' Nel waved her arms and the bangles on her arm jangled. 'All this mess, it isn't on! Absolutely everything is going to change.'

And she was right. It did. It did all change. In more ways than I expected.

First, I spoke to the GP about my all-encompassing anxiety. She reiterated that she wasn't all that worried that the lump would be malignant but understood that given what had happened to my mum, my deep concern was making work impossible. She typed a fit note for my boss to sign me off on medical grounds until the appointment at the hospital and so I stayed at home and spent my time hiding in bed. Casey would send me little videos, small clips of all the older people from the Day Centre leaving heartfelt messages. A card arrived from Donna, in her scrawling, delicate hand, telling me that I was missed. I slid the card under my pillow so that I slept on it, the words providing comfort.

Nestled in my beige bedding, I tried to read some of the novel that I'd started around Christmas, but the sentences now split apart, the words loose and unruly. I reread a single line over and over, but every time I reached the end, I couldn't recall what it had said. I tried to read the words more slowly but that didn't help me either. Feeling suddenly infuriated, I hurled the book towards the open bedroom door.

'Ow!' said James, the spine hitting his shin as he appeared inside the doorway.

'Sorry,' I said, 'I wasn't throwing that at you.'

'It's alright, love,' he said, his tone suggesting that he didn't quite believe me. He sat down on the side of the bed and presented me with a sandwich that he felt the need to tell me he'd made himself. It appeared to be some slabs of bread, a single lettuce leaf and without spread. I didn't even like lettuce. At least he'd cut it into squares and used a plate.

'Sorry,' he said.

I sat upright.

'No, I'm the one who's sorry, James. I'm finding this impossible. I'm not quite sure what else to do but stay in bed.'

He chewed his lip. 'No, I meant about the sandwich, love. I could only find some lettuce in the fridge.'

So, we weren't actually discussing it. My tenuous health. The lump that could potentially destroy our lives. I stayed silent.

'I'm also really sorry about the lump . . .' he finally added.

James looked like he was going to keep talking. I waited but he didn't speak. Then he leaned across and gently stroked my forehead. Apart from the occasional peck to say goodbye, we hadn't properly touched in months. I stayed corpse still and stared at him. When had he started to look so tired? There was stubble on his chin and creases at the corners of his eyes. The muscles in his neck were taut and his hair was shot with streaks of grey, but his face was strong and handsome still. Slowly, he blinked.

'Sorry,' he said again.

'It's not your fault,' I said, and I wondered if the stroking felt a little awkward for him too.

James bit his lip, clasped his hands together in his lap and stared out of the window at the faeces-splattered ledge. A pair of grimy pigeons puttered past each other, their scrappy feathers fluffed at random angles, occasionally pecking at each other's necks. I was wondering if the pecking was affectionate or if the birds had simply been together for too long when James's phone began to loudly ping.

'It's Nel again,' James said. 'She keeps on texting me to ask if you're okay. It's as if she doesn't trust me to take care of you.' I briefly glanced towards the sandwich. James dropped his head. 'You can't be ill!' he blurted. 'You simply can't. I'm not sure how on earth I'd cope without you here.'

I couldn't help but wonder if the man was mainly frightened of a future with an empty fridge.

'Do you mean practically?' I asked.

I instantly regretted it. James looked at me with Pixar-wide eyes. He went to stand, the hurt flushing his cheeks. Suddenly the idea of James walking out and leaving me alone was far too much to bear. I reached out to him, entwining my fingers between his, feeling the dry warmth of his familiar palm. A hand I'd held for more than half my life. I didn't want to let go now.

'I'm sorry, James. I'm so sorry,' I blurted, desperate to take back the words, whilst simultaneously scrambling to kick the sheets aside. 'I didn't actually mean that. I'm just a mess right now and I'm not sure what I'm meant to do.'

'It's okay, love,' he said, taking a heavy breath. He slumped back down beside me, his hand still knotted up in mine. I noticed deep-grey smudges underneath his eyes, and the steep collapsing slant of his strong shoulders.

'It's just so sad,' I finally said. 'I've been looking after everyone for over twenty years. I was waiting for my life to start. But the boys are both still in the house and now I could be really ill. It isn't fair. I haven't lived.'

James stared at me intently then.

'I don't know what you mean, Sarah. You haven't lived? What were the past few decades of our lives?'

That was easy for a man to say. His life had been his own since we'd first met, and I'd only made it easier. The food cupboards were always stocked, his clothes were cleaned and he hadn't physically paid a bill in years. Even when the boys were born, their arrival barely impacted him. James still managed to sleep soundly, snoring loudly through the chaos of the fractured nights and endless cries. He'd wake up in the mornings with the sole responsibility of paying the mortgage. If he chose to pop into the pub on his way back from the office, then he easily could (and often would). I always thought my time would come when the boys eventually moved out. But here they were. Here we all were.

James's lack of recognition and appreciation for everything I ever did might explain my Lenny Kravitz crush. Nel presumed my vivid sexual dreams were because the singer/actor/songwriter was gifted with a perfect face, but it was simply that the man had raised his daughter largely by himself. I would fantasise about Lenny standing in the kitchen, packing school lunches for both the boys; fresh fruit, organic seeded rolls and healthy snacks he'd picked up from a farm shop somewhere local. I would wake up flushed, pyjamas damp – and not from lack of oestrogen.

'I've spent most of my adult life caring for this family,' I carefully explained. 'Even my job involves looking after other people. When's it going to be my time? I've always wanted more.'

'More what?' James asked, his voice weary. I could almost hear the whirring of his tired brain.

'More everything! More time alone, more travel and an art career. More time to make our marriage work. That's for a start. I could go on . . .'

'What do you mean, "to make our marriage work"? I thought that we were happy.'

James took half the pale sandwich and stuffed it in his mouth. He munched, then struggled hard to swallow. I noticed a small scrap of lettuce caught between his two front teeth. An unattractive fleck of green. Then I realised he was crying.

'We *are*,' I said, softly. 'Forget it, James. Forget that I said anything.' I gripped his hand a little harder. 'It's just the lump. It's all the nerves. I promise you that everything will be okay.'

The house smelled wrong. A couple of days later, the realisation hit me. It wasn't that it smelled of anything specific, but that it didn't smell of weed. When I got up to investigate,

Ryan wasn't in his bedroom, and his bed was very neatly made. Downstairs I could hear voices rise and fall, like London pigeons swooping over urban skies.

Creeping down, I paused behind the puffy winter coats that were hanging in the hallway, just waiting for the colder months to come again. Months I might not ever see. My husband and sons were huddled around the washing machine.

'Perhaps you just press that one there,' Ryan suggested, stabbing at the solid plastic dial.

'No, we tried that one already,' James sighed.

Olly yelled to Bo, who was sat behind them at the kitchen table, intently painting all her nails the colour of a traffic cone. She reminded me of an EasyJet air stewardess.

'You're all grown men. Just google it. This is literally what YouTube's for,' she casually drawled.

'But *could* you actually switch this on?' Olly asked her, sounding desperate.

'Of course I could. But no, I won't, before you ask.'

'Bo, we'd seriously appreciate your help right now,' James began to plead.

'These have to dry,' she said, swinging her body backwards on her chair and blowing at her hands. 'And anyway, I think it's pretty awful that three adult men can't put a load of washing on. You do know Sarah's not a maid?' They hadn't noticed I was watching from the hallway. Bo waited a few minutes more, then deeply sighed. 'Really?' she asked.

'You seriously can't work it out?' The chair scraped on the kitchen floor as she pushed it with the soft backs of her perfect knees. 'Just turn that dial to forty there and then press the button that says ON.' She sighed again, then ran a nail around the edges of each cuticle as she checked the neatness of her work. 'Olly, you'd better learn to do your washing pretty fast because I won't be acting like your mother does when we're living on our own.'

The words hit like a stomach punch. My lungs leaked air. Bo was obviously unimpressed with how I'd parented my son to date and whilst I should have been offended, she clearly had a very valid point when it came to doing washing. Perhaps I should have been like Bo for all those years, relaxing at the table with a cup of tea, allowing my family to learn things for themselves. Instead, I'd ended up with men who were incapable of washing their own clothes. I turned and sneaked back up the stairs, already making mental notes of all the things I'd need to teach my family.

Just in case I was about to die.

The list was going to be very long, to say the least. But now I had a solid plan. A purpose. A distraction. I would leave my family with a 'Life Guide', filled with clear instructions on How To Survive Without Me, in the event I wouldn't be here. I fluffed all of the pillows, then propped myself upright in bed. I opened up the sketchbook that Nel had bought me for my birthday and smoothed out the pristine pages. The paper splayed like pigeons' wings. My pencil hovered over the expanse of cream. I held the pencil there, waiting to feel inspired, trying to figure out exactly where I should begin, when a yawn escaped my mouth. The last few days of worrying had been genuinely exhausting, and the tiredness felt suddenly all-consuming.

'Be more like Bo,' I told myself, as I placed the sketchbook face down on the bedding and for the first time in a long, long time, I put my own needs first. I lay back on the soft pillows and gently closed my eyes. I'd start work on the Life Guide shortly. I really would. But first a nap.

That night I lay awake for hours. Having napped all afternoon – the nap *had* been so very good – I now couldn't sleep. The London darkness glowed behind the curtains, seeping tepid light into the room. I turned on my side. In the gloom, I could just make out the shape of James beside me. He was lying with his back to me, his shoulder rising underneath the bedding like a mountain range. His familiar snores were both comforting and grating, but as I listened carefully I realised there were other sounds. The plumbing ticking, an occasional creak of wood, the metal ducts and plywood contracting as the city cooled around us. The house creaked like old bones. *Like my old bones*, I thought. Beyond the window I heard a faint siren, and the low vibrating drone of distant traffic. The sounds of life enduring.

Quietly, I crept past the small bathroom and the boys' bedrooms and downstairs, heading to the kitchen. The inside of the fridge was sparse, except for jars of condiments. French mustard in an ochre hue, the thick texture of oil paint. Green pickles floating in clear brine. Ruby-red tomato ketchup. I turned the ketchup bottle round, wiped away an errant smear. It reminded me of day-old blood on the underside of a plaster. Tucked at the back, behind the Hellmann's mayonnaise and a jar of a pickled onions, was a lone carton of free-range eggs. I held my breath. It was likely that the eggs had all been eaten and that the cardboard case had been abandoned, the effort of placing it inside the bin, a monumental step too far for any member of my family.

I lifted the lid in the cold light of the open door. Amazingly, there were two eggs. Two perfect eggs. I scooped them out and took them in my palm. They were smooth, and different shades of gold, one far paler than the other. Inspired, I ran to grab the sketchbook and the pencil tin that I'd left upstairs, not caring now who I disturbed, but I didn't need to worry. James continued with his snoring.

Downstairs again, and out of breath, I snapped on the lights and shoved the cat across the table, nudging it towards the edge. Its body flopped and dropped onto the wooden bench with a solid-sounding thump. It hissed at me, baring its teeth in outrage, and then instantly fell back to sleep. I propped the eggs at angles and carefully chose a range of sharpened pencils. HB, 2B, dark 6B.

Sketching the gentle curves, my heartbeat slowed, my hands steadied and my mind began to quiet. I stippled, circled, crosshatched subtle shadows and shapes. The whisper-thin eggshells weren't smooth at all but textured. A thousand different pin pricks, like the pores of my own skin, breathing life in.

I sat back gazing at my sketch, feeling a flush of pride. Then I turned to the page beside it and began to write instructions.

'How To Scramble Eggs,' I wrote.

I fetched a teacup from the cupboard shelf, broke the eggs into the cup and whisked them with the sharp prongs of a silver fork. Grabbing the book and placing it beside the stove, I quickly drew the outline of the china cup, the cracked and jagged eggshells, the fork coated in slick membranes that glistened in the light. *Whisk until the yolks and whites merge into one. Remove small flecks of random shells. Then add a pinch of salt.* From the fridge I took a packet of slightly salted butter. I liked its feel inside my palm. The solid weight. The pleasing shape. *Place a pan over a gentle heat and add a generous lump of butter, about the size of two or three white sugar cubes.* I drew the outline of the pan, the small gas flames, the dial twisted, turned to low.

Inside the metal bread bin there was half a loaf of still-soft bread, each slice the blinding white colour of brand new sheets. *'Put your bread into the toaster. Butter it the second that it's done, so that the heat makes all the butter melt.'*

I tipped the eggs into the pan and then I gently folded, softly stirred. I sketched and wrote ferociously, scribbling down instructions.

And then I ate the scrambled eggs, sitting at the table in the peaceful, brightly lit kitchen, with my family all asleep upstairs. Whatever happened from this point on, at least I had a plan now. To write and illustrate a Life Guide. I ate another forkful of the golden eggs which tasted of late summer haze. Of days when everything was good. Of days that were not numbered.

'You seem a little happier, more upbeat,' said Nel, her eyes smiling. 'And you're out of bed. That's a relief.'

We were sitting in the kitchen with the back door flung wide open. A warm breeze blew in from the garden. It caught the corner of the kitchen roll so that the end began to flutter like clean laundry on a washing line.

It was only just past lunchtime, and Nel was already halfway through a bottle of white wine. I poured myself a glass and sipped. I imagined that my skull was like our windows during winter; opaque with condensation, blissfully obscuring everything outside, cocooning me at home.

'I guess,' I said. 'I have a plan. I'm going to leave them

with an art book of instructions. It's a sort of illustrated Life Guide I've been working on.'

'Oh Sarah! This has got to stop. You haven't even had a scan or seen a proper doctor yet. You're NOT leaving anyone, you hear!' You don't know that.'

She was right. Of course, I didn't know. Well not for sure. I didn't know for certain that the lump was even cancerous, but I couldn't shake the overwhelming sense that I was going to lose my family.

'You're just being daft,' Nel carried on. 'Unless you mean you're leaving Plank and moving out?'

I swear I saw her eyes brighten. They flickered like a gas flame for an instant, gleamed like road signs caught in headlights of a swerving car. She chewed the end of her left plait, crunched the soggy hair between her teeth so that it made a granulated sound. I thought about my husband. About the gentle dip between his shoulder and his neck.

'He's really started trying, Nel. He's even put a load of washing on. He didn't use detergent, but it's definitely a decent start. And he's tried to clean the kitchen with the boys.'

Nel looked around, as if she were just noticing the room where we were sitting. The dishwasher was open. The low salt icon was flashing, but the drawers were stacked with plates and bowls, the worktops clear. Even the sink was empty with the small exception of a used teabag, seeping liquid slowly down the drain.

'I thought you'd given in and done the cleaning by yourself.'

'No, the boys did this. It's not too bad and I even had a coffee brought to me in bed.'

'So, it only took the fact you might be dying then?' She glanced at me. 'Not that you are!'

'I know,' I said and actually smiled. 'I guess it's almost, almost worth it.'

The cat had jumped onto Nel's lap and was gently paddling at her thighs. It tipped its head, looked up at her and she stroked its back.

'You know, I thought I'd like the break from work, but a part of me is missing it.'

I was thinking specifically of Casey with her relentless upbeat nature and her riotous laugh. I even missed the older people. Donna in her meticulously planned outfits – the strings of glass and wooden beads that matched her knitted cardigans – and Terrence with his wicked grin.

'Really?' she asked, 'I don't know how you can miss work.' She rubbed her temples, as if the very thought brought on a migraine.

I tilted my head. 'But you love being a teacher! Well, you usually do.'

Nel sighed and began to rummage in her bag. 'Just look at this!' She opened a random sketchbook and pointed at some sort of yellow mess. It reminded me of cat sick, from the time the cat thew up the remnants of a duckling. Loose feathers on the carpet. A tiny yellow severed head.

'Is that supposed to be a bunch of ripe bananas?'

'No, it's meant to be a sunflower,' she said. 'I swear that most of them took art because they thought it would be easier than Business. Only four of them can actually draw.'

Nel took another swig of wine. A larger swig than last time.

'Take this one here. Just look at this!' she said, sounding incredulous.

I looked at the small landscape, at the primitively drawn lines depicting undulating hills and the outlines of large fluffy clouds. 'Do they really think that clouds are blue? What cloud is blue?'

I laughed and took another sip of wine. I could feel it coat the inside of my mouth and fur my teeth, but it was at least working. My feelings felt more distant. Less intense and all-consuming.

She closed the Year Ten sketchbook with a clap. 'So, tell me all about this Life Guide then. Are you filling it with drawings?'

'I'm going to teach the boys the things I haven't quite got round to yet. Not just for them, but for their future partners too. I'm worried that they won't survive in life if I'm not here.'

She nodded but she didn't try to contradict me, didn't tell me what an awesome job I'd done at parenting to date.

'Well, I'm sure Bo will be grateful,' Nel said, sounding sincere.

'Oh God, not her. I'm hoping Bo is just a phase.'

Nel frowned as she carried on stroking the cat who was now blinking at her lovingly. 'You know, I think that Bo and Olly might work out. I think she might be permanent. You should probably just say sorry.'

'I know,' I groaned. 'I know I should.'

Laughter burst from Nel. The cat frightened and jumped away. Nel shook her head, her soggy plait swinging.

'I shouldn't laugh,' she said, catching her breath. 'It's just so hard to actually picture it. The argument, I mean. You never lose your temper. You're far too nice!'

'Perhaps I'm not that nice really,' I said. 'Perhaps deep down I'm actually awful.'

But Nel just laughed again and waved my words away as if they were ridiculous.

Nel was right. I did need to apologise to Bo. Also, my fingers ached from drawing and instead of feeling like a sanctuary, the house had started feeling reminiscent of the 2020 lock-down. I was having awful nightmares that it was time to join the nation doing morning star jumps with Joe Wicks. I shuddered at the memories of my wobbling flesh, Jo's tight man–bun and my single pair of leggings that seemed to shrink over the months.

Bo agreed to join me for a walk around the park. She wore a small crop top over a pair of faded baggy jeans. Her torso on display was tanned and taut. I pulled the waistband of my trousers up, stretched my T-shirt down towards my knees and tried to summon an apology as I focused on the concrete straight in front of me. There were scattered stains from chewing gum, where endless feet had pressed the tacky paste into the ground, leaving small white circles everywhere as if it had been raining bleach. A mother up ahead pushed a toddler in a pushchair weighed down with numerous canvas totes. When the toddler dropped his blanket, the mother wearily bent to pick it up.

*It all starts here*, I thought. *Before you've had the time to blink, you'll be folding all his boxer shorts and hand washing his new girlfriend's bras.*

We walked towards the boating lake, crammed with plastic pedalos in the shape of giant unicorns, obscene white swans and green dragons. There was an island in the middle which teenagers would wade out to on hot summer nights, braving broken glass and submerged cans, to sit amongst a patch of scraggy foliage with large bottles of cheap vodka. It was an urban version of *The Famous Five*. Or judging by the noise some nights, *Lord of the Flies*.

Now, the island was entirely empty, except for scrawny

London wildlife – pigeons, ducks and geese. A dog began to bark somewhere, and the birds replied in a cacophony of frantic sounds. I watched the sunshine catch upon the water, splashing light onto the surface. Around the lake were ancient trees that had survived the ever-spreading concrete sprawl. I sat down on an empty bench.

'So,' I finally said.

Bo hugged her knees and waited, tapping at her Air Force Ones with her neon painted fingernails. 'So,' she echoed, awkwardly.

'I'm sorry, Bo. I really am. I never should have sworn at you,' I blurted out. I was coming to the realisation that I'd have to share my eldest son with Bo, at least for the time-being, and I had to make things right. 'I'm really not myself right now,' I tried. 'I'm just so nervous, Bo. The lump. And well, my mother, she . . .'

A breeze was moving through the trees, drawing silky patterns on the surface of the lake. The water rippled lazily as I pulled apart the colours with my eyes. Raw sienna and burnt umber. A touch of sepia and graphite grey.

'I know,' Bo said, 'I understand.'

We sat together in silence. A group of youths still in school uniforms with Nike backpacks came screeching past, pulling wheelies on their mountain bikes. Black blazers flapped, white shirts flew loose. They reminded me of a flight of London pigeons.

'I didn't ever know my mum,' Bo said after a while. She let go of her knees and scuffed at the concrete with the toe of her white trainer. 'It's always just been me and Dad. He tried, you know. But I wish I'd had the chance to meet my mum. You're the closest person to a mother that I've got, Sarah.'

I clasped her hand and bit the inside of my lip. How could I not have known that Bo had never met her mother? I tried recalling if I'd ever asked about her childhood. Or asked her anything at all, beyond what she'd done at work that day or what her plans were for the weekend. Olly had mentioned that Bo's mum had died but I'd never pressed him for the details, perhaps not wanting to find common ground between the two of us. A wave of nausea hit me. I clearly wasn't the good person that I thought I was.

'I should have said something before,' she carried on. 'Told you just how much you really mean to me. The months since I've been living with you while we save up for a flat, I've felt cared for, like a daughter. So, I wanted to say thank you.' Her voice unfurled as soft as kitchen roll. The quilted type that costs far more.

I was caught off guard. Unprepared at how the conversation was unfolding. At her vulnerability and depth. For the first time since the boys were born, I let myself imagine a different version of my life where James and I had had a daughter. I squeezed Bo's hand a little tighter.

'I don't want to die,' I said, shocking myself, surprised that I was sharing how I felt with Bo.

We stared ahead and watched a couple on the lake struggling to steer a giant garish dragon. They were peddling frantically, laughing whilst they moved around in giant circles.

'You're not allowed,' she said, so quietly that I very nearly missed it.

'You know, I really want to be a grandmother. Not yet, of course, but some day in the future. Now I'm scared I'll never get the chance. Just like my mum.'

Bo hesitated. 'Do you think your mum's in heaven?'

I looked up towards the cloudless sky, which was the colour of the gas flame on the kitchen stove, and shook my head. 'I'm not sure I believe in it,' I said. 'I think that death is nothingness and that the life that we are living now is all we have.'

And it was the truth. It's what I thought. I didn't believe in second chances. I had absolutely no faith in an afterlife. Which made it even more incredible that I chose to mess this one life up.

On the day of the appointment at the one-stop breast clinic, I refused to let James come with me despite his many protestations. James was terrified of hospitals. The pungent antiseptic smells, the eternal claustrophobic corridors and all the illness made his heartbeat race and stomach churn.

Instead, I'd taken Nel with me.

I left her in the waiting room, swinging her feet as she tilted backwards on a plastic chair. She had turned up at the hospital with her head wrapped in a bright headscarf that was tied up in a complicated knot. She clearly hadn't thought this choice of clothing through. The people in the waiting room kept glancing over, throwing stares, their eyes flooded with pity, presuming it was Nel who was the patient.

The lady who did the mammogram was petite and young and very kind.

'Have you had a mammogram before?' she softly asked.

I shook my head.

'I'll talk you through it step by step, and it won't take long. So, left one first,' she said and smiled.

'Great,' I said and tried to smile back at her, despite the fact that none of this was all that great.

'Can I?' she asked. She eased me gently towards the huge machine, guided my hips towards the left, manoeuvred me. 'A little further forward please.' She gestured at my bare left breast, and I nodded, allowing her to take it in her freezing hands, collecting flesh before she plopped it on the ledge like a fillet of supermarket cod. 'Now put your left arm here.'

Confused, I lifted up my right, but she carried on adjusting me, deftly moving both my arms about until I was wrapped around the white machine, embracing it, my face tilted and pressed up close against the cold and curving plastic.

'Ready?' she asked. 'You might feel some slight pressure.'

I inhaled sharply. My breast was like a garlic clove, pale and roughly peeled, being crushed inside a giant press.

'Sorry,' she said. 'I'm not sure why we say that when we all know that it isn't true.'

The machine spat out strange noises as it X-rayed my flattened chest. I held my breath and closed my eyes until it was all over. Unclamped finally, I rubbed my breast, trying to ease the ache away.

'Well, this is fun,' I said, and forced a noise that was intended to be laughter but sounded like a child with croup. She smiled politely, busying herself with body parts and the precise placement of limbs.

After the mammogram I was taken for an ultrasound. This radiographer was glamorous and pregnant and was wearing bright red lipstick. I closed my eyes, too terrified to watch the screen that loomed beside the ultrasound machine and would shortly show a dark and empty dangerous space that everything would fall into. My own black hole. I blinked and shook my head, trying to interrupt my thoughts with sudden movement.

'Are you okay?' the lady asked. My palms were wet and the pores beneath my armpits were emitting damp, despite the flapping, airy gown. My heartbeat echoed in my skull. I wanted to tell this stranger I was terrified. Instead, I simply bit my lip. She nodded very gently, her understanding an unspoken thing. 'Come on, let's get this over with,' she kindly said.

Her voice was steady and composed. She patted at the paper towel and I lay down on the gurney. The paper rustled under me. Reclining in the semi-gloom I couldn't help myself; I yawned.

'If this wasn't quite so nerve racking, I think that I could sleep right now,' I said, embarrassed by my own body.

I was suddenly exhausted, as if I had expended too much energy attempting to stay anxious, a feeling that I'd felt for days.

'I take it you're a mum, then. Only mothers ever say that they could sleep in here.' I nodded yes. 'How old?' she asked whilst slowly spreading gel onto the probe, her eyes fixed on her monitor.

'Nineteen and twenty-two,' I said.

'Months?' She asked, not waiting for an answer. 'Wow! Two under two must be full on. So, I take it you adopted then?'

'No.' I shook my head. 'I'm fifty now! Those ages are in years.'

She laughed a deep and generous laugh. 'Oh God! I thought it would get easier by then or at least a bit less tiring?'

She began to calmly rub her bump and smiled that serene and naive smile that first-time pregnant women always seem to have. She was clearly pleased to be expecting and the truth would be no help to her.

'Sort of,' I finally said.

In retrospect the days when both the boys were small enough to lack free will and be constrained inside car-seats were pure bliss, but I swallowed down the thoughts that were now threatening to coalesce as actual words, stories of the things she had to come, tales she wouldn't want to hear. I smiled instead and wondered if I should have sent fifteen-year-old-Ryan off to rehab.

Throughout the scan I closed my eyes and focused on my breathing.

Breath in for seven.

Out for eleven.

I counted the numbers up and down. My heartbeat hammered in my chest, the sound like a pneumatic drill.

'This was much more fun when I was pregnant,' I whispered in the darkness as she applied more gel and began scanning the other breast. She pressed harder into my flesh, and I could hear her clicking at her keyboard. I imagined her taking measurements of the cancerous lump.

'All done,' she said efficiently, and I nervously opened my eyes. She smiled at me politely, put the probe away and handed me a wad of crunchy tissues. Her plastic gloves snapped loudly as she pulled them off. I noticed that the light that leaked from the monitor was catching at the curved edge of her wedding ring and refracting round the small box room. 'You can get dressed now,' she said, as I began to mop the gel off both my drooping breasts. The wad of tissues was nonporous, and the wiping simply moved the gel, leaving a sticky layer across my skin. I watched her face, searching for clues, trying to find in her expression some confirmation of the cancer I was certain that she'd seen, but her face revealed nothing. 'If you take a seat outside again, the doctor will see you shortly.'

In the waiting room Nel was reading a large book on bees. I slumped down in the plastic seat, laid my head on her shoulder. She tipped her head on top of mine. The aroma of a perfume that I couldn't name clung about her like an aura. Nel told me once Coco Chanel said that a woman without perfume had absolutely no future. I wish I'd worn perfume more.

'Thanks again for coming, Nel,' I quietly said.

I fixated on the scuffed and battered skirting board, the only thing not painted in a shade of pink.

'Always,' she said. 'How did the Spanish Inquisition go?'

'The mammogram? Like torture. But I didn't give my secrets up.'

'That's because there's nothing to confess!' she scoffed

loudly. Nel lifted her head, and broadly grinned. 'You haven't done a single thing that's bad enough to be kept secret since the early to mid-nineties. And if anyone should know, it's me.'

'I have!' I said in mock protest.

A woman sitting opposite with a copy of *Hello* spread open on her lap looked up, whilst slowly sipping water from a corrugated plastic cup.

'Like what?' Nel asked.

My mind became an empty space devoid of thoughts and my face flushed pink. The woman was openly staring now, clearly waiting for my answer.

'Well, I made our family move out of that flat we loved just to get the boys into a better primary school.'

Nel frowned at me and loudly groaned. 'You see?' she said. 'You're just proving my point. I love you but you're far too good.'

'By good do you mean boring?'

Nel patted my knee and said nothing, which said it all.

I scrutinised a badly painted mural of a dandelion head, the seeds all floating off across the pale pink wall towards the window that was sealed shut, whilst Nel went back to reading. She slowly turned another page.

'Did you know that bees mate in the air, and then the males lose their sex organs and die?' Nel sounded happy at the finding of this gruesome fact. 'Their penises are ripped right off, and their testicles explode and then they fall out of the sky!'

'Why all the violence and gore? Why don't the male bees just quietly die if they're not needed anymore?' I asked.

Nel shrugged and we stayed quiet for a while. I was imagining the remnants of small, detonated testes falling through the air like gently drifting dandruff flecks, when my phone vibrated with a message. I saw Ryan's name and loudly groaned. Nel peered over my shoulder.

'Is there a way to fix this?' Ryan had typed.

Three dots appeared, then disappeared, as we waited for more details. Then a photograph arrived and filled the screen.

'Oh God!' said Nel, who laughed out loud, closing her book. 'Are those Plank's shirts?'

'Not anymore,' I said and sighed, whilst staring at the photo of the once-white shirts that were now pink, the same shade as the waiting-room walls.

A voice rang out. 'Sarah Fernby?'

I startled in my plastic chair and dropped my phone.

'Is there a Sarah Fernby here?'

'Wow,' Nel whispered, loud enough for everyone to hear. 'She sounds like me at school.'

I forced a smile, thinking of Nel's stories of the infamous year tens who were apparently horrific and hormonal, all struggling with break-ups, breakdowns and ketamine comedowns.

'I'm here,' I called, waving a hand over my head, as though I was chasing a London cab in rush hour. I leapt up quickly, gathering my things and Nel, and rushed after the nurse who strode ahead. Nel and I hurried to keep up. I focused on the heels of the nurse's fast-paced feet. She stopped abruptly by a door with a small name plate: *Dr E. Duggs.* I pointed at the sign and laughed, a crackly, high-pitched laugh.

'Are you okay?' the nurse snapped with annoyance.

'The name,' I said. 'It's funny given what the doctor does and where we are.'

Nel began to laugh then too. 'My friend knows a urologist called Dr Pecker. I wonder if a name can somehow influence your fate?' she said.

The nurse shook her head. I looked down at the badge pinned to her vast expanse of chest and saw her name was Beatrice.

'So, what does Beatrice mean?' I asked.

'The one who makes you happy,' she replied, her expression like cold custard.

Nel began to laugh again as I bit my lip and forced my hands down far into the pockets of my trousers, trying not to join in too. My fingers found an old tissue, one that had clearly been subjected to a wash cycle. Compacted. Hard as bark. A lump. I stopped smiling.

Beatrice shoved the door open. Inside the small consulting room was a doctor sat at a desk, his sleeves rolled up.

'Hello,' he said.

Nel pushed me hard, propelling me into the room. I gripped my bag before me like a shield.

'Do you prefer to be called Sarah, or should we call you Mrs Fernby?' the doctor asked, reading his notes.

'Sarah is fine,' said Nel, answering for me.

My hands were shaking now, and I was sweating.

'So,' I said, just wanting this to be over, 'I know that it's bad news. It's fine. Just tell me.'

The doctor clicked his biro on and off as he studied his computer screen, and I imagined he was sending a morse code. Some frantic SOS: *Send help.*

He looked at me.

'Sorry?' he asked, as if I'd gone off script.

'You can tell me I have cancer. It's okay,' I said, trying to help him out. 'My mother did. I know exactly how this goes.'

'Sarah . . .' Nel said, but I didn't hear what she said next.

I was about to understand my fate and I suddenly felt terrified. My palms were sweating heavily now, and my heartbeat hammered in my chest. Outside the buildings loomed like a large mountain range. I imagined far-flung snow-capped peaks peeking out above soft clouds and a silence that was absolute, a place that I'd much rather be. Then a siren from an ambulance sliced through the city soundscape and massacred my thoughts, bringing my attention back into the room.

'I'm happy to tell you that you're absolutely fine,' he said, clasping his hands and looking pleased.

I shook my head, failing to fully hear him, a part of me refusing to believe him. His words were tumbling through my brain. 'Sorry?' I said.

'Both the ultrasound and mammogram were clear,' he said.

'So, it's not cancer?' Nel asked.

'No,' he said, shaking his head. 'It's not cancer.'

'Oh, thank God. Thank God for that.' Nel reached across and squeezed my thigh. 'But the lump?' she asked.

The doctor kept his eyes on me. 'That dense area that you can feel is simply normal breast tissue. We can safely leave it where it is. It's quite usual for the breast tissue to change during the menopause. Fibrocystic changes are actually very common in a woman of your age.' He rubbed his close-shaved chin as he carried on explaining. But I wasn't listening anymore. His mouth continued moving, but all that I could think of was the fact I didn't have cancer. I suddenly felt lighter. My shoulders dropped. My breathing slowed. I still had time. I had more time. I gazed beyond the doctor and stared out of the window, overcome with happiness. A single pigeon soared across the cloudless sky.

~

I spent the journey home imagining my family and searching for the perfect words to tell them the good news. I hadn't called them from the hospital, wanting to tell them all in person. In my mind I saw their faces flooded with relief, their eyes lit up with pure joy. I closed my eyes and could almost feel their tight embrace, but I couldn't help but worry about James.

Recently I'd seen a hint of everything we used to have. A growing spark. A candle glowing in the matrimonial dark. It was there each time he caught my eye and when he touched my hand in passing. This morning, when he'd said goodbye, he'd even cupped my face as if I were a precious thing, something special, to be savoured, and a part of me was scared that I might lose that, that I'd lose him as I'd just begun to re-find him.

Standing on the doorstep I fumbled for my house keys, then shoved the front door open with my shoulder blade. Inside, the hall was dark and blissfully cool. I hung my handbag on the banisters and threw my keys into the wooden dish, the one containing all the keys that were random and unlabelled, mysterious things that had stayed with us through house moves just in case they turned out to be needed. The cat came up, got in my way, walked in front of me, then to my side, as if trying to herd me, and for once I didn't really mind. Instead, I bent and stroked its ginger flank before I headed to the kitchen.

I found Olly salting water for some pasta and James standing with the clean container from the dishwasher, placing spoons and knives and forks into the corresponding compartments in the cutlery drawer. It reminded me of a plastic toy the boys both had as toddlers, which required them to place some simple plastic shapes into small holes. James was staring at a spatula which had clearly thrown him off his game.

'The other drawer,' I automatically said, 'the one below the microwave.'

'Sarah!' said James. He raced across the room and threw his arms around me, then he kissed me firmly on the lips. His chin felt rough. A day's worth of fresh stubble felt like a sheet of medium-grit sandpaper, and he smelled slightly of salt and sweat, of musk and man. Of my own man. I breathed him in.

I looked around the kitchen. It was sparkling, spotless, orderly. Someone had placed a large glass vase I'd never seen before on the centre of the table. The tulips were a deep maroon, the petals plush and darkly blushed, mixed with fronds of pastel-tinted garden peas. Olly was chopping ripe tomatoes without pulling some sort of face.

'Are you okay? How was it, love? We've all been waiting for you here at home.' James's voice was grim with apprehension.

'Don't worry, Dad,' said Olly. 'Everything will be okay. Whatever they said,' he gently told his father. Olly looked to me.

'We're so worried, Mum. Just tell us please?' Ryan chimed in.

I almost smiled then. To hear how they all loved me. To see that they were worried and that they genuinely cared. I remember that I felt as if my heart was swelling in my chest. Expanding with the power of my family's words.

'Then hopefully things can all go back to normal,' Olly said.

'Yeah, I liked things how they used to be,' Ryan sombrely agreed.

I froze at that. I held my breath. Perhaps my news wasn't that great at all. Not being sick was undeniably brilliant but it wouldn't be that long before things returned to how they used to be. The boys would stop trying around the house and James would stop paying attention. He would lose himself in work again. I took a breath, bit the inside of my lower lip.

'Umm . . .' I started talking.

The kitchen door flew open suddenly and Bo hurried in looking concerned.

'How did it go?' she asked, panting. 'What did they say?'

'At the hospital?' I asked, fiddling with my wedding ring. I rotated it in circles.

The four of them stared, waiting. There was a quiet lull that felt as if it lasted forever as my thoughts turned quickly over. I took a breath and began to speak without thinking, without knowing what it was that I would say.

And that was when it happened.

When I did the truly awful thing and told the truly awful lie.

The thing that led to all of this. The start of losing my whole family.

'The doctors don't know what it is,' I said, my heart racing. 'I had to have a biopsy today. I won't find out the results for a few weeks.'

# PART TWO

# Just a Few More Weeks

'I've done something truly awful,' I remember telling Nel the following day.

We were in the main part of Nel's light-soaked flat, which was on the third floor of a 1930s building, and consisted of a small kitchen and a living space filled with mismatching antique wicker chairs and a snug two-seater sofa. The walls were painted ivy green and covered with Nel's favourite lino prints and other art works that she'd found in vintage markets. There were tealights on the kitchen shelves and a curry simmered on the stove. I could smell the cardamon and cumin seeds, the turmeric and ripped mint leaves. Nel turned the stove down low and moved aside a cushion embroidered with a multitude of different coloured threads so that we could sit together, side-by-side.

'I know you, Sarah. I doubt that it's that bad,' she kindly said. Her laugh sounded like wind chimes.

I fiddled with the tassel of a blanket that was draped over the sofa arm.

'It really is,' I solemnly said.

Nel's brow furrowed and her eyes narrowed as she scrutinised my features.

'So, what exactly have you done? What is possibly that awful?' she asked, clearly unconvinced that I'd done anything of interest.

'I couldn't cope with the idea that things would all return to normal. I just need some time to work out how to make the changes permanent, to keep my family from returning to the way things were before. I can't go back. So, I've told them that I might be sick and that the lump could still be cancer.'

I blurted out the words and waited for Nel to say something, but she didn't speak. Instead Nel laughed. A great big belly laugh that seemed to start down low, and rippled up her body, spreading in waves along her limbs until she was consumed. Her earrings jiggled joyfully, until suddenly her face fell flat. Nel had realised that I wasn't finding any of this funny. In fact, I hadn't even smiled. I chewed the soft flesh of my lip.

'Oh God, Sarah. You're serious? I thought that you were kidding. Please tell me you're not serious?'

I said nothing. Nel switched the flickering gas stove off and then downed a gulp of water at the sink. She put her glass back on the kitchen worktop with a thud. I watched the water slip and slide. A small, contained tsunami.

'But your family must be so concerned, and Plank would know. How on earth have you convinced him that you had a needle biopsy? You would have a wound.' Nel looked perturbed. I could almost hear her mind crackling as it raced through the logistics that my lie involved.

'Well, I've stuck a plaster on my boob,' I quietly said.

'You've done what?' she asked, her voice sounding incredulous.

I pulled down my top, tugged at my ancient flesh-toned bra and showed her the small plaster that I'd found inside the cupboard underneath the sink. The plaster looked ridiculous and, despite Nel's disapproval, a flicker of amusement finally crossed her face.

I held my breath.

'You're going to hell!' she slowly said, her eyebrows raised. 'I always thought I'd go alone. I guess at least I'll have some company.' She shook her head and looked perplexed. I wondered if the movement was helping her to rearrange the way she'd always seen me in her mind. The honourable friend. The honest one. The good and moral mother.

Then we spoke about the fact that my one little lie would only be for two short weeks, until the imaginary biopsy results arrived. It wasn't that long, especially in the context of a lifetime. I assured Nel that it wasn't a big deal and that it wouldn't cause my family any real harm.

Nel seemed deeply unimpressed with me.

'Breast biopsies are common now. I think they're practically routine these days – I mean I did well to avoid one – and I doubt that James or either of the boys will be too overly concerned.'

'I guess,' Nel finally said, her voice softening. 'I mean, a lot of women that I know have had some sort of lump assessed. I suppose it's not unusual.'

'Exactly! And anyway, it's not for long. Two weeks is hardly any time and by that point the boys will be more used to doing things around the house. I'm hoping they'll have formed some really good habits. Ones that actually stick. And James and I . . .' I trailed off and shrugged both of my shoulders which made the plaster on my breast pull.

'You and James?' Nel prompted. She stood up as she was speaking, and moved to her small kitchen sink, filled a tiny metal watering can. She paced the room, adding water to her spider plants and trailing ferns, her line of hanging hoyas. I watched Nel as she stroked the leaves and palpated the damp soil with her fingertips. I watched the slim shape of her back.

'Everything's been better since he heard about the lump,' I said. 'It's like my husband's finally noticed me again. I feel like he sees me, and I've missed that. I've missed having his attention.' Nel's back flexed as she stretched to reach a terracotta plant pot, beside a lump of dusty rose quartz, on the highest kitchen shelf. 'I think he really does love me. I've been worried for a long time that there was nothing in our marriage left to rescue, but I think this lump has made him realise just how much he cares and I'm not ready to give that back.'

'But James has *always* loved you,' Nel said, turning towards me.

I shrugged.

'It's only been a couple of days but I just keep having these moments where I feel truly awful. I mean I've never told a lie like this before. But I think the extra time will help, and it's not as if I've told my family that I'm definitely about to die. I've just left things uncertain.'

Nel was quiet for a moment. 'I suppose,' she said, sounding unsure.

And so, I let myself believe that what I'd done wasn't too terrible. I convinced myself the lie I'd told was for the best. That I was helping my whole family, by giving myself time to turn my children into better human beings and time to set my marriage on a better path. I was lying but for good reasons.

At home that night I cooked dinner, a meal I'd made a million times. I pulled fresh thyme leaves off the stalk with a firm pinch of my fingers and chopped them with a sharpened knife. The room filled with a woody scent. The chicken was stripped of plastic wrapping and its dignity. It lay exposed without its feathers in the cooking tray, its skin covered in goosebumps. I crammed it with two lemon halves, split garlic cloves, and drenched it with golden glugs of olive oil, a generous pinch of cracked sea salt and a feathering of fragrant thyme. Potato peels spiralled from my hands and I tucked the creamy potatoes into the hollow spaces in the tin, forming a pale and starchy halo.

Olly appeared and leaned against the door frame. His cheap suit jacket was compressed inside the angles of his arm. There were sweat patches staining his shirt that spread from both his armpits. He wiped a hand across his forehead.

'How did selling houses go today?' I asked.

'Really good,' he said. His face lit up. 'I showed this couple a flat just now. It's in a different league, Mum. There's even heating built into the bathroom floor. I think they really liked it.'

I still found it incredible that I'd birthed and raised a human being who found the concept of warm floor tiles quite so exciting.

'Are you sure you should you be cooking, Mum? Shouldn't you be resting?' he said, looking suddenly concerned.

'It was just a biopsy. I promise that I'm fine,' I said. Because I was. I was completely fine. Sickeningly well.

I felt so guilty in that moment, and I found myself craving

the feel of his hand when he was young. I closed my eyes, remembering his little fingers curled tightly up in mine, safely cocooned. The silken skin, the warmth pulsating in my grasp, as if his fist were an extension of his small and beating heart.

'Do you want to help me cook?' I asked instead. After all, this was the very reason that I'd lied.

I handed him a carrot and the ancient plastic peeler. Olly looked confused.

'Like this,' I said. I grabbed another carrot, swept the peeler blade away from me so that orange ribbons fell like party streamers, forming piles on the worktop.

I should have taught the boys when they were small. The first and only time I ever tried to cook with them was an attempt at simple fairy cakes. There was flour trailed through the house, white powder piled everywhere. The boys got bored, especially with the weighing part and cooking part and waiting for the cooling part. They ate the cakes still oven hot, the buttercream all melting into sticky pools inside their palms. I was left to deal with the chaos of the kitchen, a house coated in fingerprints and two children on a sugar high. I never baked with them again.

Olly cracked open a beer can from the fridge, took a gulp and sighed with satisfaction before he poured me a large glass of wine. He began to peel the carrots like I'd shown him and then he chopped them into little discs. As the carrots simmered gently on the stove, and the chicken crisped inside the oven, Olly fiddled with the Spotify app on his phone, linking Bluetooth to the speaker. Suddenly the room was filled with pulsing sound, and I moved an empty chair over and leaned my back into the spindles. I smiled at my adult son who was choosing to spend time with me and for a moment I felt less guilty, convinced the lie was for the best.

'Can you write down all the timings for the chicken?' Olly asked. 'Bo would love it if I cooked for her.'

'Of course I can,' I said gently.

My hands left damp marks on the thighs of my voluminous, baggy trousers that I'd bought because the waistband said 'all sizes', allowing me to avoid selecting the right size, a size I'd rather not acknowledge. I reached to grab my sketchbook, which was lying beside the fruit bowl and an overflowing vase of coral-tinged carnations. Flicking through the pages I found the illustration of the chicken that I'd carefully drawn. Small pencil arrows pointed to the temperatures and cooking times. Olly put his beer can down and scrunched up his eyes.

'Can I?' he asked.

I handed him the sketchbook. He thumbed the pages, taking in the sketches and the accompanying instructions. His movements made the warm air dance. He looked at me, his eyes asking a question.

'I've wanted to do something for both you boys, since . . .' The words merged with the music.

'Since you found the lump,' he finished for me, nodding. 'In case . . .' he said.

Olly swallowed very loudly and focused on the sketchbook. He stopped at a page covered in illustrations of small origami folds, beside the heading 'How to wrap a present or a parcel.'

'Mum. This is really, really beautiful.' I remember that he sounded shocked. He turned a page and ran his fingers over carefully drawn contours, the stipples, hatches, crosshatches.

'Thank you,' I said, rotating my wine glass by the stem, my face flushing with alcohol and pride.

'I had no idea that you could draw.'

'Really?' I asked, 'You know I have a first-class arts degree from St Martin's. Aunty Nel and I, we both went there.'

'I know you do. I mean I know you studied there with Nel but it's just – I've only ever heard stories. They didn't ever feel that real to me, and I've never seen your work before. I've never actually seen you draw.'

The music filled the pauses, and my fingers tapped the drum beat out on the wooden kitchen table as Olly peered intently at more pages. How had I never allowed myself to draw in front of him? What had died in me and when?

'This wouldn't just help us, you know. Ryan could start a

Pinterest page for you or an Instagram account. You honestly should share this, Mum. He's really great at all that stuff.'

'He is?' Surprise altered the cadence of my voice.

'Is what?' asked James. I startled, turned to see my husband standing in the kitchen door. He was home earlier than usual, never normally here in time to eat with us. The cat was stuck like Velcro to his dark grey socks, purring as it rubbed its flank against him. James didn't wait for me to answer but walked towards the oven door and peered through the glass. 'That smells so good.'

I watched him, really watched him as he stood there staring at the back end of a stuffed chicken. His shoulders were much wider than they used to be, his body broadened over the years. He dropped his head towards the ground, tucked his chin into his chest to stretch his spine. His tie was tight around his neck, a fabric noose, and he wrangled with the awkward knot, his fingers moving frantically. He looked so very tired and as the knot loosened, my heart strings pulled.

'Do you want a beer?' Olly asked him, getting up, heading towards the fridge.

James turned, surprised, and caught my gaze. Our son was being thoughtful. As Olly handed James a can of ice-cold Heineken my husband clapped a hand on his shoulder. Olly wrapped an arm around his dad, and they squeezed each other tightly. They stood there like a solid wall, both leaning up against each other whilst the music thrummed a background beat and we basked inside the evening warmth, the softening light. For a fraction of a moment, I let myself believe that everything would be alright. Even better than alright, perhaps. Just how deluded can a person be?

The back door was wide open. Beyond it, the laundry on the drying rack had crisped under the sun after being left outside all day. Now, the stiff clothes moved like cat flaps. I closed my eyes, imagined bright Tibetan flags, kaleidoscopic fabric prayers that fluttered under distant skies.

Only James and I were left sat at the table with the chicken bones still in the roasting tray. I ripped a fresh baguette apart, dipped soft bread into the juices, mopped up the sticky fla-vours that had pooled into the corners. Moisture dribbled down my fingers and I sucked the oily goodness from each individual fingertip, my lips smacking. James took a ravaged chicken thigh and teased out the meaty remnants that both the boys and Bo had missed. As he reached to take another swig of frosty beer, his hand brushed mine.

I felt a warmth spread through me, which was probably just the consequence of the current London heatwave, the wine and a severe shortage of oestrogen. I was thinking that some coffee and a cool shower might be a sensible idea when James reached and cupped my face inside his hands. He gazed deeply into my eyes.

'Sarah …' he said, his voice low, as if my name was steeped in meaning.

'Mmmm,' I managed somehow.

He leaned in close. I closed my eyes, and I felt our lips connect. The alcohol took over and we kissed like we were teenagers, both searching out the crevices of each other's mouths. He tasted of sweet garlic, chicken, fragrant thyme and the man I used to know as mine.

'Come on,' he said, taking my hand as I blissfully surrendered to the moment.

The cat looped itself between our shins as we stumbled up the stairs. We shut the cat outside the door and ignored its yowls of protest. I fell onto the bedding as James fumbled with his shirt buttons, his eyes filled with a longing that I hadn't seen in years. I flushed and made sure that the plaster on my breast was firmly stuck in place, as James wrestled with his underwear. My body was his nourishment. Despite the dinner we'd just had, the man in front of me looked starved. It was only me he wanted in that moment. James wanted me.

Afterwards we lay together in the twilight, our limbs intertwined. My head rested against his chest, and I could hear his heart beating beneath his ribs, a steady thrum.

'I love you so much, Sarah,' he whispered as he ran his fingers gently down my forearm, linking moles together with his touch to create a path that stretched across my skin. The lie I'd told had been worth it if only for that moment.

'I love you too,' I murmured back, my heart swelling.

The sound of his calm breathing felt like something close to solace.

'Hang on a sec.' He gently moved me across the bed, pulled on some clothes and disappeared. I lay in the fading light, naked with the sole exception of a slightly faded sports bra and a plaster on my right breast which was threatening to become unstuck. I pressed it flat. Willed it to stick. My body buzzed, endorphin soaked as I listened to the city sounds that merged into the background of our daily lives. There was music playing in a garden somewhere further down the street, diluted wafts of conversation that were interrupted frequently by sharper shrieks and barking laughs, and the screeching of a car alarm.

'I'm back,' James said, closing the bedroom door carefully behind him. He was grinning like a cat that had just got the cream, or more precisely like an adult who had just had sex for the first time in a long, long time. The cat slipped in and curled itself into a corner, licked its paws and cleaned its ginger ears.

'I can see you're back,' I said, bemused.

'And look at what I found!' he said. James was holding out a tiny plastic bag of what was either oregano from the kitchen or dried marijuana buds. In his other hand, he had rizlas and a lighter. 'I stole these out of Ryan's room.'

This made oregano less likely.

'But we don't smoke.' I said. 'I thought you disapproved.'

'To hell with rules right now. Life's far too short.'

A shadow briefly passed across his face. My palms prickled with sudden damp.

'What do you think?' he asked, oblivious to my guilt. There was a hopeful note inside his voice. 'Shall we?'

'At least open a window,' I said. As he leapt towards the sash window, I dragged myself to sitting. Then James placed the bag of buds and papers on the bedding right in front of me. He sat cross-legged on the mattress and looked at me expectantly.

'I can't roll up,' I said, pulling in my chin as I realised what he was asking.

He frowned. 'But I thought that you and Nel had wild youths?'

'Compared to you! And anyway, it was mostly Nel. But she always found some random boy to roll her joints.'

The YouTube clip was helpful. The woman was American, with an accent that was professional, and her nails were neatly manicured, the tips whitened like crescent moons. She sounded far too sensible to be smoking weed and she made the whole thing look so easy. It turned out that it wasn't. Her joint was thin, a perfect thing, whereas ours looked like a tampon for a woman with a heavy flow. We began again, and I soon found I was laughing at how ridiculous we must have looked.

'Pause it!' I cried, still chortling, struggling with a new attempt as the woman's hands moved far too fast to follow.

Eventually we had something that was bent and warped but didn't crumble in our hands. I held the joint between my lips, rolled my thumb across the lighter until the spark became a steady flame. The joint glowed like a setting sun as I took a drag, and the smoke began to scratch inside my throat.

'Are you okay?' James asked as I spluttered and coughed, my lungs alight. I took a sip of water and nodded a 'yes', batting the smoke away.

'No, I mean, about the lump, Sarah. Are you okay?'

I squeezed his hand and shook my head, took another slow, protracted breath and exhaled a cloud of smoggy fumes. As I smoked, my brain began to quiet and my body started melting, my muscles merging with the mattress. Lying back against the pillows I watched the particles of dust flicker and gently flit, the dying light catching the lint. I couldn't think of what to say. I didn't speak.

'I understand,' he softly said. 'We don't have to talk about it now.'

He took my hand and kissed it as he told me for the second time that day how much he really loved me.

'I love you, too,' I said, passing him the joint. And I did love him. I truly did. But you're not supposed to hurt the ones you love.

On Thursday evening I told my family that going back to work would take my mind off things and that I missed the people at the Day Centre. The truth was that I couldn't bear to stay at home. I had been off work since Monday and there was nothing wrong. I wasn't ill. I wasn't even worried that I could be ill. It had also transpired that having too much time alone, drawing in my sketchbook, reading magazines and watching mindless trash on Netflix, wasn't quite as fun as I'd imagined when I'd had no time. The house felt far too empty, and I felt useless. Especially now the house was clean, the dishes done, the garden neat.

'Well, only for tomorrow,' James had said, smiling. 'I've been speaking to your manager. Sue agreed you can take next week off.'

'You have? She has? But why?' I asked, my voice panicked. My lungs had turned to concrete, and I spoke too fast, the words thick in my arid mouth. I imagined all the things James might have said to Sue. 'I think it's better that I work. I'll go mad at home.'

'Just stop worrying,' he said, coming round behind me, kissing my neck. 'I promise that you'll love it. We're doing something really special.'

But I was worried. I didn't want to lie to people who weren't family. I'd sent Sue a short email on the day of the appointment to say that I'd be coming back and promising to fill her in with all my news on my return. I'd planned to thank her for her patience and her kindness and to share the fact that I was well. I hadn't ever thought through a scenario where James would speak to her before I did, where my worlds of work and home would mix. My pulse quickened.

'So, what exactly did you say?' I asked. My thighs felt damp.

'It's fine, Sarah.' But his smile fell.

'It's not,' I said, 'It's really not. I haven't even told her yet.'

'About the biopsy?' he asked. He looked confused.

I dipped my head.

'But why?' he asked.

'I just . . .' I paused, needing more time – more time to think. I breathed out sharply through my nose. 'I haven't told her yet because I doubt there's anything to tell. It's probably just a normal lump. You know it isn't that unusual, James. Women find lumps all the time. And I don't want to take more sick leave. It isn't fair. They'll have to pay my salary as well as forking out for someone else to cover my shifts.'

He patted the air, trying to calm me down.

'It's fine,' he said again, his voice level. 'It's okay, love. I haven't told her anything at all and you won't need to take the time off sick. She said you haven't used up any of your holiday this year.'

Relief cascaded from my open mouth. I didn't want work's understanding or their misdirected kindness. I didn't deserve any special treatment.

'I know,' I said. 'Because we never go away.'

James pretended that he hadn't heard.

'That's settled then,' he said smiling, as if he'd won an argument I hadn't realised we were having.

'What are we doing, anyway?' I asked, my eyes narrowing.

'It's a secret,' he had said, grinning.

*Well, we both have those,* I thought grimly.

I took the sketchbook with me on the bus to work. In fact, I took it with me everywhere. What had started as a way to stay distracted from the lump was now a new obsession, or a renewed obsession. I'd forgotten just how much I'd always loved to draw and now that I'd begun again, I didn't want to stop. I loved everything about it. The feeling of the pencils as they moved across the page. The way the world melted away as I focused on the details. The sense of calm and purpose that creating brought. I could transform a white and empty page into something beautiful, with the extra benefit that I was creating something for my family. A handbook for their lives.

As I walked into the Day Centre, I tucked the sketchbook and the pencils in my bag. The pencil stubs felt like old friends, an extension of my fingers. It struck me as ironic that the pencils which I loved the most were the most battered, destroyed from wear and overuse.

'You're here!' a voice called out. Casey threw her arms around me, pulled me into an embrace. She smelled of honey and fresh coffee beans.

'I am!' I said, glad to be back, to be somewhere where I didn't have to lie. Here I could tell everyone that I was well.

'Does that mean you're fine? What did they say?' she whispered, looking serious.

But before I had a chance to speak, we were interrupted by Terrence. He was shuffling fast across the room, Donna walking close behind him. I remember Donna wearing pearls. Small perfect spheres that looked like they'd been carved from teeth. Terrence had even found a comb somewhere and had neatened his unruly hair, trying to look respectable. Casey gently squeezed my shoulder as she pulled away and rearranged her face into a grin again.

'We missed you, Sarah. So, so much,' she said a little more loudly. 'It's not the same place here without you.'

And it wasn't only Casey who had missed me. It seemed that everyone was pleased that I was working once again. They all seemed genuinely thrilled to see me. I could hardly recall how that felt.

'You okay, love?' Donna asked later that day, her forehead creased with deep concern.

The two of us were sat together at a table, looking out over the car park from the bay window. The sun that day was glorious, and the asphalt sparkled in the light.

I nodded.

'I don't want to pry, but I overheard Casey and Sue. They were chatting whilst you were away and I didn't mean to eavesdrop on their conversation, but they sounded really worried about you. I hope that everything's alright. Are you okay?' She rubbed the swollen knuckle of her thumb, massaged the joint stiffened by time.

'I'm fine,' I said. 'I'm really fine.'

She tipped her head and looked at me intently with her age-glazed eyes so that I felt compelled to keep talking, to fill the space.

'I just panicked. It was stupid. I found a lump and for a while I thought that I was really sick. But it turns out it was nothing.'

'That's good to hear. I was worried for a while there. Having cancer is no joke, you know. I had it once,' she said.

'You did?' I asked. Surprise seeped through my words.

Donna was wearing a smart shirt dress in a muted aquamarine, the fabric printed with pale taupe flowers, and the leather of her handbag matched her dress. I looked down at my shapeless uniform, the tunic top too baggy, the fabric a loathsome shade of pale purple. Donna pursed her lips, moved a jigsaw piece around, pressed the piece into a waiting space.

'Oh yes,' she said. 'But years ago.' She waved her bony fingers, dispelling the memory into the air. 'God, I really can't stand jigsaws . . .' Her eyes flitted across the little pieces laid out face-up on the tabletop. A picture broken into parts, pulling at our human need to make things whole. 'I'm glad that you're okay though. I really am.'

She picked up a piece of bright blue sky, examined it. Casey flitted past us carrying a cardboard box of different-coloured hats, a feather boa coiled loosely on top. She made the air move as she passed, and the hem of Donna's dress danced as though caught up in a summer breeze. I was quiet for a moment as I sorted through the jigsaw pieces, unsure what I was searching for.

'I was so terrified that I'd die soon.'

Donna gave a loud laugh at my words. She looked around the room at all the people who were clearly going to die shortly, their skin sagging, their limbs feeble. She took my hand in her own.

'Oh, darling girl. I have a strong suspicion you'll outlive me.' She smiled to herself as she pressed the little piece of sky into an empty waiting space.

Later that day I found Casey in the staff room. Casey didn't want to be a carer and whilst the older people loved her energy, this wasn't what she'd dreamed of doing with her life. In the years before I'd found the lump, I'd always felt a little jealous. At only thirty-two she still had time to change direction. She could make it as an actress still. She was always at auditions, and she was positive that it would just take one. One lucky break. She remained relentlessly upbeat. Now her face was puffed, mascara streaked.

'You left this by the kettle,' she sniffed. 'I'm really sorry. I knocked it off the counter when I went to get a cup of tea. It landed on the floor, open.'

In a trembling hand, she held out my sketchbook and then began to fumble with her mobile phone and I caught sight of the camera app closing. There was a photo on her screen of one of my drawings. Her cheeks flushed pink, and I wondered how I could have been so stupid as to leave the sketchbook lying around.

'Did you photograph my drawings? Those are personal,' I said, trembling.

I shook my head, feeling increasingly incensed.

'You said the lump was nothing!' she blurted out, not answering my question. 'But you've made this for the boys and James. You must be dreadfully ill, Sarah. You just didn't want to tell us.'

'Casey, I'm fine,' I said firmly, my anger seeping through the words.

Casey just cried. 'Of course you're not. Why else would

you have made this? You're just lying to protect us,' she said, refusing to believe me. 'You're always putting other people's feelings first. But if there's anything that I can do . . .' Another sob caught in her throat. She looked so forlorn.

'Casey—' I tried, the anger dissipating, but she caught me up in a fierce embrace, the sketchbook caught between our bodies. She stood back and held it out to me.

'This is truly beautiful, you know. It's a real piece of art, Sarah. You should be so proud.'

Before I had a chance to say another word, she fled from the room, rubbing her tear-filled eyes.

I didn't follow her. I didn't move.

A part of me was angry that she'd been snooping and had photographed my sketches, but I was also thrilled she'd liked them. The approval of my sons was great, but to have my artwork praised by someone who wasn't a member of my family sent pleasure coursing through me. I should have followed after her. I should have gone and found her to explain. But the truth is that I didn't.

'Morning! Do you want some coffee, Sarah?'

I was standing in the kitchen two days later in my pyjama bottoms and an oversized T-shirt that I think belonged to Ryan. The kettle that had recently been matt and dull and crusted with limescale was shiny now. As the water started boiling the kettle wobbled, shaking in its stand.

'Yes, please,' I said. 'Thanks, Bo.'

'Sorry?' She cupped her ear with her right hand.

It was hard for us to hear each other. It wasn't just the kettle that was on. The washing machine was revving through the final minutes of a wash cycle, and the drum was churning with a roar that made the cupboards shake. We waited for the death rattle of the final spin, before the machine slowed into stillness.

'Yes, please,' I repeated. 'That would be great.' I watched Bo fill a coffee mug and take a carton of oat milk out of the fridge that I didn't recognise and hadn't shopped for. I shook my head.

'Cow's milk is fine. One sugar, please,' I added.

'Oh no, Sarah. I don't think so. That's really not a good idea.' Bo vigorously shook her head and poured oat milk into my cup. The tea turned grey. 'I've been reading up on diets and I know it isn't certain you have cancer, but sugar is absolutely terrible. And cow's milk is packed with hormones which are especially bad for breast cancer.'

I forced a smile and took my mug, as Bo helped herself to a generous splash of cow's milk. I watched her add a single spoon of sugar and stared at her with envy.

'Who put the washing on?' I asked.

'Oh, James did that before he went. He left a note.'

She handed me an envelope that contained our latest bank statement that, for once, James hadn't opened. He usually ripped it open the precise second the post arrived to scrutinise the month's spending. Then he would file it away inside his colour-coded ring binders that he kept neatly inside a drawer. But on that day, the envelope was still sealed shut, and James had written on the back. I traced my finger over the words which flowed across the white paper.

*'I hope you have a lovely day. You need to pack for somewhere hot. Bring clothes to last you for five days. We're leaving in the morning!'*

I couldn't help myself. I grinned. It wasn't exactly poetry. Not a love letter, nor thoughtful prose. But it was everything I'd wanted. I started to imagine all the places we might go. A city break in Paris. Or perhaps even New York. Or a villa with a pool somewhere.

'That's so exciting!' Bo exclaimed, reading the note over my shoulder.

She sat down at the table with a thud and brought me back into the present. She munched through a large mouthful of white toast smeared with Nutella. Crumbs scattered across the tabletop. The cat appeared and started licking up the crumbs as Bo scrolled through all the recent photos on her camera roll and selected one. The photo was of Bo wearing a sports bra and some shiny Lycra leggings. She was pouting in the mirror, her body arched, her breasts puffed out. She cropped and tweaked, chose a vibrant filter for effect, added some text and held the screen out for me to see: *The only awful workout is the one you didn't ever do.*

'But you don't work out,' I said, confused.

I took a sip of tea and shuddered at the taste.

'I know,' said Bo. 'I hate the gym. Honestly, I look like this without trying.'

I resisted the strong urge to roll my eyes. 'Of course you do. You're twenty-three!'

'I know.' She frowned. 'I'm getting old.'

'But claiming that you exercise – that's lying, Bo.'

'I suppose,' she said. 'It's crazy, right? But it's only a white lie.' She took another generous bite of toast.

I didn't have the right to comment on her lie. I scanned her youthful body. I'd never had great breasts like hers. At twenty-three mine had been considerably smaller. Back then I survived on cigarettes and vodka, and despite the jutting hip bones I was still worried that I looked too large. As I watched Bo eat her chocolate-covered toast, I wished I'd eaten much, much, more.

'And anyway,' Bo carried on. 'The truth won't help my followers. My job is just to motivate them.'

She stroked the cat and the needy lump of fur and bones purred loudly whilst it stared at me with narrowed eyes.

'Your followers? How many of them have you got?'

'Ummm,' she said, clicking refresh on her phone. 'I'm almost at eighty thousand followers now.'

'Eighty thousand? Eighty thousand living people?' I screeched so loudly I disturbed the cat. It scrambled up and arched its spine until its body formed the shape of an inverted toilet u-bend.

'I really help these people, Sarah.'

'How?' I asked. 'Exactly how? By pretending that you're someone that you're not?'

She shrugged. 'I'm *inspirational*, Sarah. Just think of all those people who are healthier because of me. Does it matter if I don't work out?'

Bo stuffed the last corner of toast into her mouth and then handed me her phone. I watched as the post began to gain a stream of miniature love-hearts, endless likes and a list of grateful comments.

*'You're an inspiration to us all.'*

*'GURLL – so damn hot.'*

*'I needed this. Off to the gym!'*

'But . . .' I stopped myself. I had no right. The lie I'd told was so much worse.

'Sometimes,' she said, sucking Nutella from her fingers, 'the truth isn't what people need.'

As I handed Bo her phone back, I looked around the kitchen. All the cupboard doors were neatly closed, the fridge well stocked and the worktops immaculate. Pink carnations splayed out from a water jug, adding a vibrant burst of colour to the room. Flowers that I hadn't bought.

And then, there was the fact that I was finally going on holiday somewhere overseas. I hadn't had to book that, either. It was everything I'd hoped for. So, I swallowed down another sip of grim, grey tea and forced a smile. *Sometimes*, I repeated in my head, *the truth isn't what people need.*

James flew me to Ibiza on the Sunday.

When he presented me with the tickets, my whole body shuddered with anticipation. It was somewhere that I'd always dreamed of visiting. James didn't even make us take the train but ordered us an Uber to the airport without once mentioning the cost. 'Where is my husband and what exactly have you done with him?' I joked.

At the check-in desk at Heathrow the man behind the counter, with the smart neck scarf and suit jacket and small enamel name badge saying 'Gavin', presented us with a suspiciously swift upgrade to business class.

'Oh God,' I said, turning to James, my face flushing. 'You didn't tell the airline all about . . . ?'

'No!' James stammered quickly. 'I haven't mentioned anything about your breasts.'

In silent horror, Gavin and I competed to see which one of us could turn the deeper shade of red. Gavin won. He awkwardly explained that the upgrade was on offer because the flight was overbooked that day. Then he busied himself with the labels on the suitcases.

'There's a lounge upstairs you're free to use,' he said,

presenting us with boarding cards, looking relieved that we were leaving.

Initially it seemed that business class wasn't all that different to economy, with the small exception that we got to board the plane first and our seats were situated in the second row. I read the seat numbers and frowned.

'Oh,' I said. 'I think that they've messed up somewhere. There's a stranger sat between us.'

But apparently, that wasn't the case. According to the flight assistant, in business class the middle seat on short-haul flights stayed empty. More money bought you extra space, distance from your spouse. I reached across and took my husband's hand. Now, I wish I'd sat beside him and held on longer.

The plane taxied to the runway, then propelled itself into the air. I placed my sketchbook on the middle seat and drank the gin and tonic that was offered only moments after take-off. James scrambled for his wallet, but the stewardess waved away his card and handed us a small packet of pretzels each.

James soon fell asleep. His jaw fell slack and his head tipped back against the seat. Re-circulated plane air whistled through his nostrils and his open mouth.

As he slept, I peered out of the window. The sky was Prussian blue and beneath there was a thick layer of un-dulating, pale clouds. They were soft as sage, the colour of fresh milk. Even the clouds were magical, looked down on from above.

I sat flicking through the sketchbook. It was nearly full of sketches now. Soon it would be finished. There were pages filled with recipes and a whole section on DIY. I traced my fingertips across a spread that I'd filled with different screwdrivers and the tools required to fix things. Small drawings of a flat head, Phillips and a Torx, the lines all neat and perfect and the shadows sharp. I held the pencil over an illustration of a drill. The sunlight bouncing off the clouds caught in the corners of my eye. It was impossible to concentrate. All I could think about was how much my life had changed in a few weeks. The husband that I'd thought had checked out of our marriage was sleeping peacefully beside me as we flew business class to Ibiza. It was hard to fully comprehend.

James woke up half an hour later, rubbed the stiffness in his neck and yawned. He reached across and squeezed my thigh.

'I can't believe we're doing this,' I said, my voice filled with excitement. I bit my lip. 'Are you sure we can afford it?'

James nodded and swiftly looked away.

'But how?' I asked, suspicious that he wouldn't look me in the eye. 'You always say we need to be more careful with our spending and that there isn't any money spare.'

James started fiddling with his wedding ring. 'It's not that we don't have money,' he eventually said, looking down towards his lap, his voice quiet. 'It's just that I've been putting a small chunk away for us each month. In fact, I found a market-leading rate. A three-year fix at 4.32%. The deals that are out there if you . . .' He began to sound excited, and his words sped up, but then he noticed my intense silence. 'I'm sorry. I did it for the both of us. The money was supposed to be a fund for our retirement, you know, to top up both our pensions. But now that you might be really sick . . .' He trailed off.

I stared at him. My eyes narrowed. I stared harder. A fury grew. It felt solid, barbed and its heat expanded deep inside me.

'Are you telling me we could have gone on holidays?' I hissed, the words like arrows.

'Umm . . .'

'Or eaten out in restaurants? Or replaced the ancient microwave that is probably irradiating all our cells?'

He looked at me in horror then. I sat entirely still, staring back at him, refusing to avert my gaze. The experiences and things that we'd missed out on, the sacrifices I'd made – unknowingly, unwillingly – ran riot in my brain, haunting me, the ghosts of things I'd never had, would never have.

I didn't have the right to be so angry that he'd lied to me. After all, the lie that I was telling was much worse, and it was partially my fault that I knew nothing of our finances.

Years ago, before the boys were born, James and I had lived together in a tiny, rented flat above a mobile phone shop on the Euston Road. Initially we'd shared it all – the cooking and the cleaning and the paying of our monthly bills, despite the fact that James was earning more than me. My art degree had left me largely unemployable, and I'd been working at the snack bar in the local cinema, bringing home a paltry wage. But then I'd fallen pregnant, and whilst the other pregnant women seemed to glow, I'd felt like death. James had taken over everything. He'd been successfully promoted and arranged a mortgage with the bank, so that we could move into a proper home. After the boys were born, I could have shared more when it came to managing our finances, but the truth was that I'd been so busy with our children and the numbers never really interested me.

Or so I'd thought, until now.

I downed my gin, feeling my brow furrow.

'I . . .' he tried.

'Don't you think you should have asked me first? Wasn't this the sort of thing that should have been decided by the both of us? At the very least, there was a proper conversation to be had. I can't . . .'

The flight attendant appeared again with the drinks trolley, almost as though she sensed my urgent need for alcohol. I leaned across as if James wasn't there. She poured the gin and using tiny metal tongs filled another plastic cup with oversized ice cubes and a dainty little lemon slice. The whole process took an uncomfortably long amount of time. I took the drink and turned my body to the window, nursing the glass against my chest.

'I'm sorry, Sarah,' James said, his voice coming from behind me. 'I only did it to look after us. But you're right, I should have talked to you. Can you forgive me?' I felt his palm against my back. 'Please?' We're together and on holiday, and if you do have cancer like your mum . . .'

He stopped talking and after a moment I felt his hand retract. I heard him fiddle with the buckle on his seatbelt and I briefly glanced around to see him walking down the narrow aisle towards the toilet with his shoulders slumped. I sipped my gin, the taste clean and botanical, whilst James stayed locked inside the toilet for a concerningly long time.

'Alright?' I forced myself to ask when he returned.

'I feel truly awful. I'm so sorry.' He reached across to take my hand, but I pulled away and turned back to the window.

James had done well with the booking. The hotel wasn't large but it was truly luxurious. There were sunbeds all around a pool, a cocktail bar and a small al fresco restaurant complete with giant parasols shading linen-covered tables.

Our suite was on the top floor with a view over the azure sea. A lady from reception beamed as she showed us the small safe inside the wardrobe and how to turn the aircon down. The floor-to-ceiling window was almost totally obscured by helium-filled red balloons. The bed was scattered with fresh rose petals and the bath towels had been carefully twisted into two swan shapes, their bills touching. The empty space left a large heart.

Once she'd left, I turned to James and raised my eyebrows. He held his hands up in surrender. 'Before you even ask, they have no idea about the lump,' he said.

I glowered at him.

'Sarah, I wouldn't tell them that you're waiting for results. That's personal.'

I tore open the envelope propped beside a silver ice bucket that contained a complimentary bottle of champagne. 'Congratulations,' was written on a card in a neat and curling font.

He came to read over my shoulder. 'Fine,' he said, voice sullen. 'I may have said that we got married to make sure that we got a lovely room.'

I slumped down on a corner of the pristine bed and fiddled with my T-shirt hem. Despite myself, I laughed.

'Well, it worked,' I said. 'And I guess it's not a real lie.'

'No,' said James. 'I mean it's true that we got married. Just a frighteningly long time ago.'

We were married in 2000, on the twentieth of January, and for months before the wedding no one was entirely convinced that the world would still exist by then. People worried the turn of the millennium would cause the entire world to melt down, technology incapable of dealing with a year ending in zeros. Networks would crash, planes would fall out of the sky and the world would turn to chaos.

None of those things happened and Nel was deeply disappointed, because it meant the wedding went ahead.

Our honeymoon was a long week spent on Dartmoor, in a room above a tiny pub. In my imagination the place was going to be idyllic. Romantic, English, deeply quaint. James and I would spend our days together walking on the wild moor, wrapped in hats and padded coats and knitted scarves, admiring the impressive drama of the views, and building up an appetite. I had even planned to draw and paint and had packed my favourite watercolours. In the evenings we'd return hungry and windswept to curl up together in the pub with local pints and well-cooked food. But it rained all week. Torrential sheets of slanting grey, a graphite shade. The bed sagged in the middle and the bathroom reeked strongly of damp, with a bath that made you feel dirty, and not the kind of dirty that's ideal for a newlywed.

I looked around our hotel room now, with art on the walls, feather pillows on the bed and an iPad on the polished desk. The screen showed the current temperature outside. A blissful twenty-nine degrees.

James went over to the ice bucket and soon I heard a cork

pop. The noise momentarily reminded me of home, of a car engine backfiring in a distant London car park.

'I didn't mean to hurt you, love. The money … it was meant to help us in the future. I shouldn't have …'

He passed me a champagne flute. The champagne bubbles effervesced. I focused on the tiny spheres of moving light that darted upwards, moving increasingly faster as they rose.

'To us?' James asked, holding out his own glass.

I looked around the hotel room, at the helium balloons, the crisp white king-sized bed covered in sheets that I hadn't had to launder and I raised my glass.

'To us,' I said, and at last I smiled.

I went over to the balcony and heaved open the thick glass doors without thinking. A breeze lifted the red balloons, and the helium-filled hearts escaped. James came to stand beside me and we watched the hearts disperse into the cloudless sky until all that we could see were tiny pinprick dots. His fingers searched for mine and I finally let him take my hand.

It was early afternoon, and James and I were lying by the swimming pool. Our London tans were terrible. We both had dark bronzed forearms, and my calves were tanned from wearing three-quarter length culottes, but our bodies were a luminous white. Nervously, I removed the airy cotton Kaftan that Nel had lent me for the trip and ventured to the poolside, the tiles emitting so much heat that I was forced to walk on tiptoes.

James joined me where I sat, dangling my legs, swinging them in circles through the water. I liked the feeling of resistance. The way the water on the surface was fragmented by the movement of my limbs and broken into bright patterns. There was a vibrant shimmer, vivid shine. Tugging at the shoulders of my swimsuit, I tried to pull the whole thing up.

'Wow, the biopsy has healed well,' James said, sounding so pleased.

I looked down to where the plaster had peeled away, at the skin devoid of scars, and managed to somehow mumble, 'Yes.'

James slid into the cool water, dipped beneath the cobalt surface with his sunglasses still on. They floated gently off his head and then slowly sank towards the bottom of the tiled pool. I lowered myself down off the poolside and dove beneath the water, using strong and rhythmic strokes to pull myself under. The sensation was delicious. I retrieved the sunken sunglasses, and kicked my legs, propelling myself upwards to the surface like a mermaid with a penchant for potatoes. As I went to hand them back, James pulled me through the water, as if I were weightless, a waif. I wrapped my legs around his waist and found that he was kissing me. His mouth tasted of mint toothpaste, and he smelled faintly of coconuts from the factor fifty lotion he was slathered in.

'I'm really glad we're here, Sarah,' he said, his arms gripped tightly round my waist. 'I promise that I won't keep things a secret anymore. We'll decide together what we use our money for. I promise, love.'

Balancing his sunglasses back onto his head I kissed him deeply once again. He briefly spun me round and round and I laughed just like I did when we were younger, when the world felt truly magical, mysterious and full of good. I was genuinely happy in that moment. I was finally on a holiday, with no children, and at home I had a tidy house and time to draw.

Dinner was divine that night. Almost as amazing as the shower in the hotel room which had the largest shower head I'd ever seen and water pressure that I'd previously only dreamed of. The waiter told us that he'd been informed we were on honeymoon and had reserved us the best table, a corner booth with cushioned seats and candles and some privacy. The air had cooled, and my arms began to goosebump, and I shuddered. James disappeared, quickly returning with his favourite jumper, which he draped around my shoulders.

The last time James had been this attentive was when we found out I was pregnant with Olly. He had fussed about and pampered me, excited by the prospect I was growing us a human using half his DNA, but the novelty wore off as soon as I gave birth. When I fell pregnant with Ryan two years later, James seemed to be living under the insanely wrong assumption that it was easier the second time around, as if practice somehow made the whole process of pregnancy less challenging. The fact that I was dealing with bad morning sickness, a torturous lack of sleep and an energetic toddler, one who really hated nap times and had recently developed a proclivity to biting everything and anything (but mainly human flesh), seemed to somehow pass my husband by.

Now, we clinked glasses and congratulated ourselves on finally making it away on honeymoon to somewhere far more glamorous than Devon during the winter. Even if it had taken us almost three decades to get there.

'So,' James asked. 'What would you like to do?'

'Right now?' I asked between mouthfuls. I was spooning large heaps of paella into my mouth. The saffron soft rice was crammed with slivers of squid and topped with silky roasted peppers. The dish was close to perfect.

'I'd like to eat the rest of this,' I said. 'Then have dessert.'

James laughed and motioned to the waiter, asked for two spoons and picked out three desserts from the menu.

'Three?' I asked.

He gave a deep nod. 'Three. For us to share.'

Soon, three desserts were placed between us. I took a

large forkful of cake, which tasted of sweet almonds. There was a glistening bowl of ice cream and a small dish of crème brûlée too. We ate until we couldn't take another bite, then ordered two black coffees.

Above our heads the sky had turned an inky black and myriad stars were splashed like celestial confetti across the Spanish sky. I leaned far back to take them in and sighed with satisfaction. James brought his chair over next to mine and rested his head against my shoulder.

The waitress brought us two brandies.

'On the house,' she said. 'The staff think you're adorable. Such a great couple.'

James reached for my hand and tightly squeezed.

We came home to a spotless house. The cat was fed, the counters clear.

James and I stood in the hallway with our luggage, as I gazed around.

'Is this our house?' I asked in an awe.

For a start I hadn't tripped over a pair of random trainers or an errant Adidas backpack or another of Bo's handbags, which seemed to multiply like gremlins that had been fed just after midnight. I remember that I'd felt fantastic, happy that the boys were learning how to be good human beings. Reliable. Responsible. Men who knew exactly how to clean.

There was only one more afternoon before my fictional

appointment and then my family wouldn't need to worry anymore. I was really looking forward to no longer having to lie to them but was equally determined to relish the few remaining hours. I was thoroughly enjoying my temporary vacation from reality, but I knew I couldn't let it show. After all, my family thought that the next day I would find out if I had cancer. It was essential I seemed worried, but pretending was exhausting and so I decided to avoid them all.

Unfortunately, it seemed that they had other plans. Bo and the boys had obviously decided that the best thing they could do for me was to ensure I was distracted. They refused to leave me on my own. They hovered like a cloud of flies. I suggested that I go unpack, but even that wasn't allowed.

'I'll put your washing on for you,' Olly very kindly offered.

He was wearing baggy tracksuit bottoms that were probably once grey but were now the same off-white colour of London snow and all my cotton underwear. It was strange to see him in the kitchen, during daylight hours. Olly was usually hiding in his room, smoking joints out of the window, only venturing downstairs at night to make himself some toast. If I had to make a candle that reminded me of home before I found the lump, it would smell of marijuana, soap and jam.

'And I'll make you a fresh smoothie,' chimed in Bo.

Bo's voice sounded too bubbly, too impossibly upbeat.

'Oh, no thank you. A coffee would be great though,' I said.

I was dreading more grey oat milk, but any form of coffee was an improvement on a smoothie.

'About coffee …' Bo slowly said. She twirled a length of glossy hair around one finger and pulled the sort of face that I usually reserved for squeezing out portions of wet cat food. Her skin shimmered like cleaned Perspex and she smelled of sherbet sweets and the packs of pastel-coloured highlighters that I used to covet as a child. 'I've been doing some more reading.'

'Oh …?' I asked with hesitation, filled with genuine dread.

'Coffee is bad idea.'

Bo began to pour a heaped spoonful of flaxseeds and some broccoli stalks into the see-through blender jar.

I watched in abject horror.

'But I might not even have cancer.'

She fiddled with one earring and shrugged, which made her tank top rise, revealing the fine outline of a tattooed crescent moon.

'Exactly! You might be just fine, and if you are, we want to make sure that you stay that way. Which means an anti-cancer diet from now on.'

I inwardly groaned as she began to tell me all about the hidden powers of vegetables and the abilities of grains and seeds to fight cancer and lower my risk of heart disease. Bo began to rattle through a long and incomprehensible list of foods that I could and couldn't eat now, some of which I'm certain that she had confused. Mid list, she flicked the blender switch to on, drowning her own voice out. For sixty perfect seconds there was just the sound of pulverising vegetables. I watched the vegetables gyrate, green solid forms swishing at speed, until their shapes turned into gloop.

The evening was considerably more pleasant than the smoothie. The boys wanted to watch a movie as a family, something that we hadn't done in years. Olly and Bo were trying to convince us that *John Wick: Chapter* was a cinematic masterpiece whereas Ryan wanted to watch *Mad Max*. No one could agree, until James suggested that, for once, I choose the film.

'Yes, come on Mum,' Olly cajoled.

'That's fair,' said Ryan, gravely.

My family settled on the sofa, and all stared at me expectantly. This was a moment I'd been waiting for. I had no desire to watch their films, but they wouldn't like mine either. So armed with the remote control, I flicked through all the options, until I found what I was looking for.

'*Kung Fu Panda?*' Ryan asked. His hair fell flat across his forehead. It moved like a sheer curtain. 'Mum, I don't know if you've noticed but we're no longer twelve,' Olly said.

'Well, it used to be your favourite film. And it's my choice.'

Ryan loudly groaned until his older brother kicked him with the back part of his heel, forcing Ryan into silence.

Twenty minutes later my family were all staring intently at the screen. Bo, Olly and Ryan were sharing the large sofa, Bo's head resting on Olly's chest. Even Ryan wasn't fidgeting as he watched the animation. They were clearly all entranced and I remember the warm feeling – a mixture of nostalgia and contentment. We were sitting there together as a family. All because of me.

The next day was 'results day', for results that didn't exist, arriving on a date that I had fabricated.

Nel had promised that she'd come with me, to hang out in the hospital, as I pretended to find out the news that I was fine. But then I got a text from Nel. I asked if she was panicking unnecessarily or if it really smelled that awful. She told me to imagine rotting oysters, decomposing prawns and a slab of month-old salmon, all abandoned in the bottom of an outside bin in August.

'Really?' I typed, my nose scrunching at just the thought. I'd never had the opportunity to eat an oyster in my life, but I understood the general gist.

'It also looks quite frothy. And it feels like everything's on fire.'

The contents of my stomach churned as I wondered who she'd slept with now.

I assured Nel that I'd be just fine and that it might be sensible to find a sexual health clinic that would accept an urgent walk-in.

'I'll come instead,' James said, steeling his voice. 'I want to be there for you, love.'

I stared at him. He was struggling with the button on his collar. 'It's just another building. I can be inside a hospital. I mean, I'm a grown man and it's not like I'm a patient there. We'll both be fine.' But his face had already turned ashen.

I couldn't risk James coming to the hospital and finding out the awful truth. The truth that I had lied to him. To all of them. I took his hand.

'James,' I said. 'I love that you would come with me, but you really hate the hospital and I'd rather go alone.'

'There's no way . . .' he began.

'Just imagine if you panicked and you couldn't bring yourself to stay? It would cause a scene.'

The fingers on his other hand started tapping, measuring out his anxious heartbeat on his trousered thigh. I realised that the buttons on his shirt weren't lining up and that his collar looked bent and askew.

'But . . .' he tried again.

'And I need to worry about me today. Not anybody else.

I should be done by two o'clock. Why don't you come and pick me up?'

He nodded then.

'If, you're sure?' he asked, the colour returning to his cheeks.

'I'm sure,' I said.

I don't know which of us was more relieved.


I headed to the Feltham Arms, an old and sprawling pub opposite the hospital. I suppose I could have waited out the next few hours somewhere else but being close to the hospital felt somehow less dishonest.

Inside there were a few tables of people – a young couple who were deep in conversation and a group of friends all drinking pints. The menu was pretentious. That day's special was 'chicken thighs with gently crushed potatoes nestled up against a compote of French spinach and fresh garlic'. Sky Sports was playing on a large flat-screen TV, which was mounted on a bare-brick wall, beneath a plastic chandelier. There were printed flyers scattered across the tables, promoting a new pub quiz on Thursday nights. I perched on a small leather stool at the slightly sticky bar and ordered a tequila and a packet of pork scratchings.

'I haven't had a shot in quite some time,' I laughed, my voice high-pitched and tight.

The barman glanced towards me. 'Are you falling off the wagon love? Because my brother, well he's in AA, and he's doing really well now. I won't forgive myself if I'm here serving tequila to a lady in recovery. Do you need to call your sponsor?'

'No. It's not like that. I just ... well I ...' He waited. 'It's just that I'm about to get my life back.'

The barman looked deeply confused as he filled my glass.

His arm was wrapped tightly in cellophane, from his elbow to his wrist.

'Did you get burnt?' I asked, trying to change the subject.

'This? Oh no. It's just my new tattoo,' he said, following my eyeline, before explaining that each major life event was inked onto his body. 'I'm like a walking Facebook timeline. You see this one right here? I got that one the day after my Granny died,' he said, pointing at a tattoo of a lily flower that spread towards his shoulder, the floral fronds like fingers. 'It's because her name was ...'

'Lily?'

He nodded, then pointed at my glass. 'Another one?'

It appeared that I had drained my drink already. I shook my head and wondered if either of the boys or any future grandchildren would ever be tempted to get my name immortalised on their own bodies. Although if they ever discovered the lie I'd told of course they wouldn't want to.

I sunk my head onto the bar, pressed my forehead against the tacky wood.

'Are you alright?' the barman asked, walking over with the bottle of tequila.

I laughed. 'Unfortunately, I really am. I'm fine actually. I'm doing great,' I said, the words escaping in a flurry. I must have sounded slightly unhinged.

'If you're sure,' he said, looking unconvinced.

He moved further down the bar and I reached into my bag to find my sketchbook. Being careful that my hands were clean, I took the sketchbook out. It was finished, finally done. The leather of the sketchbook felt familiar now, softened with time and frequent handling. I flipped through the pages, each one carefully curated. It was beautiful. The result of endless hours of work. A love letter to my sons. The horizontal hatching and the contour lines, the feathering and blending were something to be proud of and the fact it wasn't needed now made me dreadfully sad. A dying woman's guide to life wasn't useful if she wasn't even vaguely ill.

Closing the book, I gently stroked the cover as if it were a household pet about to be anesthetised. Then my phone pinged very loudly. A text from Nel:

'FUCKKKK.'

I assumed she'd added extra Ks for emphasis.

'Are you okay?' I texted back. 'Have you got some awful STD?'

I watched the three dots on my phone as she typed a

reply. They disappeared, appeared again, until eventually a text arrived.

'You need to look at Casey's Facebook. I can't chat right now. I'm about to have my legs in stirrups, but I'll call the second that I'm done.'

I clicked the Facebook app open and searched around for Casey's page. I felt my heart stop beating in that moment. I couldn't breathe. A high-pitched ringing filled my ears, and for a moment, I couldn't see. I blinked and it came back into my vision. A giant photo of my face beside an illustration from the book, which she must have photographed at work, and a link to a JustGiving page. My hands shook as I clicked the link and began to read:

*I've worked with Sarah for the past year. She's the most amazing woman that I know. Sarah spends her days caring for a group of elderly people at a Day Centre in North London and her free time caring for her family. Sarah has been diagnosed with breast cancer. She even went as far as trying to tell me the results were fine, because she didn't want to worry me. That's how wonderful she really is. Sarah is an artist and during this difficult time she has created a Life Guide for her sons, filled with illustrations. Her work is truly beautiful, and I'd love to raise the money so that she can see her drawings published. This would be a dream come true for her, so please give anything you can.*

I tried to think. I couldn't think. The overwhelming panic was interrupted by two women in their twenties who bustled through the pub's front door and made a beeline for the bar, their legs like cranes. The barman rushed over towards them. I watched the women tilt their pretty heads as they chatted, laughed, their arms linked. I imagined that their lives were blissfully simple. I had no idea what I should do.

I paused and took a long, slow breath. I needed to call Casey, to have a serious conversation, but my phone had already started ringing and it wouldn't stop. I stared at the familiar name. James kept calling but I couldn't bring myself to speak. The barman and the two women were looking over at me now. On the fourth attempt, I answered.

'Love, I'm on my way. I'm coming now. Bo saw the news on Facebook.' James sounded deeply frightened.

'Bo?' I asked. 'But how?'

'She's Facebook friends with Casey.'

'They're friends?' I said, incredulous.

'Yes – they met last year at that barbecue to raise money for the Day Centre. Anyway, Bo sent me Casey's post.' James was rambling, speaking far too fast.

'James—' I tried.

'It's okay. I'm a little hurt that you didn't tell me first but that's seriously not important now. I'm just so sorry that the news was bad.'

'But James—'

'Just wait right there. We'll get through this together. I love you, Sarah, I really do.' A car beeped in the background, and I heard James curse. He took a ragged breath. 'I'm driving but the traffic isn't great. Oh God. I should have come to the appointment. I'm so sorry, love. I'll be with you in twenty minutes at the latest.'

He hung up the phone, leaving me listening to the sound of my own beating heart. I sat, immobilised by fear.

I should have called Casey right then and told her I was fine. I should have made her take the post down. I also should have rung James back. But I was panicking and frightened. Adrenalin coursed through me as I willed the world to go away. I closed my eyes, pretended that I wasn't there. Nothing felt real. Or perhaps it was that everything felt far too real. My phone was still clasped in my hand, a digital grenade that could explode at any moment. My head was filled with thoughts of James. I would let him know that I was fine, I would tell him that the news was good, that the biopsy results were clear and that Casey was mistaken. James. I thought only of James.

I actually jumped when Olly texted.

'I love you, Mum. Bo and I will both help out. And Ryan too.'

I'm pretty sure I groaned out loud.

～

When James arrived, I was waiting on the pavement outside the hospital entrance, people bustling around me. My palms were damp. I watched other patients come and go and I wondered about the secrets that their bodies hid. *Other* patients. I wasn't one at all. A woman wearing a turban walked past me towards the glass revolving doors, her skin sallow, her cheeks hollow. I swallowed down the bile that rose in my throat.

'I'm fine. It's not cancer,' I blurted as my husband hurried towards me.

There were people everywhere. Sharp sounds of wailing sirens. The traffic from the busy road. The collective noise of chaos. I stood exactly where I was. James glanced quickly at the hospital and shuddered before reaching out to me.

'Oh, love. I'm so sorry. I shouldn't have let you come here on your own today.'

He clearly hadn't heard me. I let him fold me up in an embrace. He felt like home. A home that I'd betrayed.

'James, just listen, please. I'm fine.' I tried to pull myself away.

'My god, you're brave.' He held me even closer. I could feel the damp heat of his breath as he whispered in my ear. 'I know that you'll be fine, Sarah. Treatment has come on leaps and bounds. There's this woman that I work with, and she had breast cancer two years ago. She's in remission now. You will be too. I just know it, love.'

I took a breath and pulled away from him. This had to stop. He had to know.

'But James, I'm—'

'And then there's this.' He handed me his mobile, open on the Facebook post. It seemed my non-existent cancer news had spread at an impressive rate, like headlice around a primary school. Colleagues from work and long-lost friends were all liking and donating at a frightening speed and leaving heart-felt messages. In the hour since the post appeared, the JustGiving fund had reached almost one thousand pounds. I groaned again. 'People are really quite amazing, and this shows you just how much they care. Have you seen what someone wrote, suggesting an exhibition? You know that could be really great. To have something positive to focus on, amongst all this.'

I stopped at that. I stopped trying to tell him then. Instead, I took his phone from him. Underneath the post someone called Kai had typed, 'Casey! It's been a while. I hope you're well. I'm not sure if you know this but I've been working in a gallery since drama school. We could potentially show Sarah's work. Could you get in touch?'

Casey had replied to Kai already: *I've DM-ed you.*

It's truly awful to admit this but all that I could think of in that moment was the possibility of an exhibition of my work. It was a dream come true. Not any dream. My wildest dream. The thing I'd always wanted more than anything. At least back then. I imagined my drawings framed and hung on gallery walls and crowds of people, solely there to see my art. It was all about to happen if I let it. If I could just steal a tiny bit more time.

'I . . .' I stuttered, trying to think of what to do.

I remember wondering if it would really be that awful if I just waited for an exhibition to take place. How much harm could waiting cause? If I let an exhibition go ahead, then afterwards I could say the doctors made some big mistake. You read about those stories in the papers. People given wrong diagnoses. Tales of poor patients who have the wrong limb amputated or the incorrect organ removed. It was rare but not unheard of. And I would return all the donations, of course I would. By then my work would be out in the world and people would feel sorry for me, thinking that I'd been put through an unimaginable trauma, being told that I had cancer when there was absolutely nothing wrong. They would feel compelled to buy my work and I could become a full-time artist. I thought about the things that had improved already in my life. My relationship. The house. My sons. Just a few more weeks wasn't that bad. It wouldn't make me a bad person. At least, I let myself believe that at the time.

'Sarah?' James asked. 'What was it you were going to say?'

'Nothing,' I said, shaking my head and threading my arms tightly around him. I hid my face in his strong shoulder as I whispered, 'Nothing at all.'

# PART THREE

# The Last Two Weeks

The boys were flat that night at dinner. Bo was tearful and subdued. We sat mostly in silence.

'Come on now, guys,' James attempted. 'We all need to stick together and be positive for Mum right now.'

I forced a smile and pushed a buttered new potato around my plate.

James's brow creased with concern. 'Aren't you hungry, love? No, of course you're not. You must be in shock. I don't think that any of us thought today would go like this.'

He shook his head, and I stared at James, bewildered. Just like everyone else, I'd had absolutely no idea that the day would end up like this. I'd surprised myself. The shock was real.

'Did you know?' asked Ryan quietly, his eyes half-hidden behind his fringe.

'Know what?' I asked, my pulse quickening.

'That the lump was cancerous? Do you think that you could sense it?'

'No,' I said. 'Not really. No.'

I stabbed the new potato and crammed it in my mouth. I tried to chew, but my mouth was dry and I couldn't breathe. Potato caught inside my throat and for an instant I imagined how much simpler everything would be if I just choked to death right then and there. But that was all just wishful thinking.

'Are you okay?' asked Olly, staring at my red and sweating face, as I forced the mouthful down and reached over for some water. Ryan thumped me hard across the back.

'Mmm hmm,' I finally coughed, nodding.

But I was clearly not okay. My family thought that I had cancer. All my friends did too. And now strangers on the internet were donating hard-earned money to a fabricated cause.

'So, what happens next?' James asked, when I'd eventually stopped coughing. 'When does treatment start? What is the plan?'

They all looked at me, their expressions open and expectant. The room was full of hopeful eyes and tilted heads. I cleared my throat.

'I can't right now,' I said. Their attention felt unbearable. I stood up fast and the kitchen chair legs scraped across the lino floor. 'Do you mind if I call Nel?' I asked. 'We haven't spoken yet today and I'm not feeling very hungry.'

'Of course,' James said, leaping to his feet. He reached out to me but I backed away. The boys and Bo watched anxiously. 'You do whatever you need to. I didn't mean to push. Take all of the time you need.'

I leaned over the banister to make sure that nobody had followed me and carefully closed the bedroom door. Collapsing in a puddle on the floor, I pressed my back against the door.

'Finally!' Nel said, answering my call. 'Please tell me that you've sorted things.'

'Not quite,' I said, and then proceeded to confess exactly what I'd done.

Her reaction was even worse that I'd expected. I knew that she'd berate me, but I'd never heard her angry. At least, not with me. Apparently, this time I'd gone too far.

'It's fine,' I said, attempting to convince her, and myself perhaps. 'It won't be for long. I promise, Nel.'

I waited for her to say something, say anything. The silence thrummed. I glanced around the bedroom, desperate for some distraction.

The bedroom, at first glance, was bland and lacking personality. But the longer that I sat there on the floor, the more I saw. Beside James's side of the bed was a large glass filled with water. Each night he'd bring a fresh glass up to bed with him and would then proceed to leave it totally untouched. There was the tiny pot of Vaseline that he used instead of lip balm, with the lid undone, the sides smeary, a jar of sealed multivitamins that were marketed 'For Men'. and a single shell. The shell was nothing special. Just a boring, basic cockle shell, fan-shaped with gently radiating ribs. I'd found it on our second date when we took a trip to Brighton and I'd given it to James on the train home. I shook my head, incredulous. I hadn't realised that he'd kept it.

On my side of the bed was a novel that I couldn't read, my brain failing to focus on the linking of specific words to form some kind of meaning. There was a small, framed photo of the boys aged ten and twelve, their arms around each other's shoulders. It was taken at a city farm and there was a llama in the background. If you looked closely, you could see the tiny graze on Olly's chin from where he'd fallen off his scooter a few days before. The boys looked slightly grubby, their hair windswept, and they were both grinning.

'Oh God, Sarah.' Nel said. 'I can't talk about this now. I've got to go.'

'I . . .' I stuttered, lost for words, unsure of what to say.

We both listened to the silence for a moment.

'Seriously, what have you done?' Nel finally said.

And I wondered yet again that day exactly what I'd done.

The next day was a Friday. I should have been at work, but I'd had a text from Sue the night before insisting that I take my time, as much time as I needed. I felt awful about not working, about letting all my colleagues down, but I decided that it might make sense to be at home so that I could formulate some sort of plan. I considered telling everyone the truth, but that didn't feel like an option. I should have done that yesterday. I'd had plenty of opportunity. But now if I said anything, my family would all know that I'd purposefully withheld the truth and let them think that I had cancer. They would be angry and appalled. The shame would likely kill me. And then there was the prospect of the exhibition that I'd always dreamed of. If I told the truth, it wouldn't ever happen. I would need to find another route out of the chaos I'd created.

I lay in bed, consumed with over-thinking. The cat came in and stretched itself across the bed, belly exposed, its eyes half closed, its body relaxed and languid. I watched its stomach rise and fall, its breathing slow and gentle. I tried to slow my breathing down to match, but my brain felt like it was on fire. I had to make people believe that I was genuinely ill. At least for the time being.

The cat shifted and began to scratch the rolls of fur around its neck. I frowned at it, so jealous of its simple peace. The first thing that I'd need to do was learn everything and anything there was to know about the different types of breast cancer, about the treatments and their side effects. I'd have to schedule times for scans and for appointments at the hospital. I'd have to be so organised. But I'd spent my life in training for this moment. I'd spent my life juggling two boys, a home, a husband and a job. I was sure that I could do this too. I'd make this work.

I'd told Donna, my favourite person at the Day Centre, that I was fine, but Donna was old, and if she said something people would probably assume she was confused. That happens with the elderly, I told myself. They mix things up.

And Nel? She was the only one who knew the entire truth. But Nel was my friend. She was practically a sister. I genuinely believed that she would bury a body for me. Even if she disapproved, I didn't worry that she'd ever tell.

I picked up my phone, intending to google breast cancer, but became distracted by an email in my inbox. From the moment Casey learned about the lump she had signed me up to some revolting online newsletter and every single day a loosely motivational quote was emailed to me. They reminded me of the messages tucked inside the fortune cookies from the bad Chinese Nel loved to order from on Friday nights.

That morning's words of wisdom were from Marie Curie's biography. According to the world-famous physicist:

*We must believe we are gifted for something, and that this thing, at whatever cost, must be attained.*

James had brought me a cup of coffee before going to work. I took a sip now, barely noticing that it was cold. I read the words again, studying them, as if they were a message from beyond intended just for me. The words were an assurance that I was doing the right thing in hiding the truth about my health until an exhibition could take place. As I reached to put the coffee down, my hand brushed up against the leather of the sketchbook, which was balanced on the corner of the table.

I stroked the cover and thought about the fact that this was exactly what I'd wanted. To be left in peace. To not be needed. To be devoid of all responsibilities. Now that everyone believed that I was ill, no one expected anything from me. I'd imagined this would feel akin to freedom, but I felt empty and lost. Staying in bed was suddenly unbearable.

I walked towards the window and threw open the beige curtains. My arms stretched out at right angles. My body crucifixion wide. A pigeon frightened from the window-sill. It stumbled for a second, shocked, then lurched away. I tracked the pigeon as it flew towards a too-bright sun. The sky was vibrant blue that day, the colour of the Domestos bleach that I used to clean the toilet with, and it was marked with vapour trails that looked like pencil lines. In the next-door neighbour's garden, their youngest child began to scream, jumping on a trampoline, piercing my thoughts.

When the doorbell rang, I was relieved. The contents of

my head felt like an enemy and I was glad to be distracted from myself.

Downstairs I found the postman on the doorstep, looking awkward and uncomfortable, holding out a small handful of household bills. I'm pretty sure the post would have fitted through the letter box. Why had he rung the doorbell?

'For you,' he said. He held the post like an apology.

'Thank you.'

I took the letters, and the postman looked down towards his hairy calves. He didn't turn to leave but loitered on the doorstep beside the giant wheelie bins. Next door's bin was over-flowing with rubbish bags and the lid was slightly open. It smelled of liquifying vegetables and the metallic tang of sanitary towels.

'Umm . . .' he mumbled quietly. He twisted his boot, grinding it into the tarmac. 'Your neighbour down at fifty-seven. She said that you're unwell. I just wanted to say sorry and to let you know you're in my prayers.'

'Oh,' I mumbled, caught off-guard. 'How does she know?' My neck felt suddenly hot and damp. The skin prickled.

'She saw a Facebook post.' He peered at me, studying my expression. 'I'm sorry if I'm not supposed to know.'

'No,' I stuttered, 'no, it's fine.'

There was a long and awkward pause. I fiddled with the letters, bent the corner of an envelope.

'My dad had cancer too!' he blurted in a rush.

He looked at me then. Dead in the eyes. I'd never felt so seen before, as if his eyes could bore into my soul and see my sins. The sensation was unnerving. My brain faltered. My thoughts stopped dead.

'Prostate,' he added quietly, and he looked back down towards his feet.

'Oh God,' I said, and I tried my best to smile gently, to sound upbeat. 'How is he now? Is he okay?'

'Not really, no,' he said. I stared at him, and he spluttered to move on. 'But I'm sure you'll be far luckier. I'm sure you're going to be just fine.'

He croaked his words as though his throat was gripped inside a vice. My smile felt like wet cement as I tried to rearrange my face into something more appropriate. He continued to survey the ground and I remember staring at the bald spot on his head. Its smooth tight skin. Its sweaty sheen.

'Oh God,' I said again, 'I'm so sorry.' And I really was. I felt as though I'd betrayed his dad, that in lying I'd abused him.

'Me too,' he said. 'I'm sorry too.'

Closing the door, I threw the post down on a table and sagged against the hallway wall and slowly breathed. My head felt full of angry bees. I rubbed my hands against my temples, but it didn't help.

The next few hours spent staring at my laptop screen

didn't help either. I was trying to understand breast cancer, but the entire subject was far more complex than I'd hoped. The language was obscure and the deeper that I went, the less I understood. There were different types, with different grades and also different stages and words I couldn't comprehend: triple negative, invasive and ductal carcinoma.

By the time I went to meet Nel for her lunch break on Hampstead Heath, my head was aching, and my eyes felt strained. Thanks to the sunny weather, the heath was far busier than usual. There were people having picnics, young couples walking arm in arm, children clambering over fallen trees and runners in their gym gear. We passed the lane that led towards the ladies' swimming pond where a small gaggle of women who looked about our age were towelling off their hair, discussing HRT.

'But I still don't want to sleep with him,' one lady said, laughing. 'Although perhaps that's not the hormones and just him.'

The rest of them began cackling and discussing how the patches all compared to pills, and the highly coveted Oestrogel, which apparently smelled awful.

'It's just like slathering on vodka. I swear its mainly alcohol. I'm concerned that in this heatwave I could self-combust,' I heard another woman say.

The buzzing in my head continued as the women walked

on past us and their chatter quickly filtered out. Above our heads, there was an archway of horse chestnut leaves, the giant fronds in shades of army-green and vibrant lime. The light flickered as the sun's rays filtered through, dappling the pebbled pathway. I felt a little better.

'Sarah?' Nel said, her voice too loud.

I startled as she said my name. 'Sorry?'

'I was saying that I think this is a bad idea. In fact, it's absolutely awful. You know that you can't keep any of the money that's donated, right? And the boys must be so worried now. And then there's James.'

I noticed that she'd called him James, instead of Plank. His name sounded so strange coming from out of her mouth. I bit my lip. It was usually Nel who refused to care what other people thought, who didn't worry about consequences. It was usually me who was sensible and serious. Yet here she was, clearly stricken with concern.

'Of course I'll give the money back! I'm not a total monster, Nel. And the boys and James . . . Well, it's only for seven more days,' I said, instead.

'That's a whole week!'

'Fourteen days tops,' I carried on. 'This woman, Lia – the one who owns the gallery – wants to take me out for lunch in town on Monday. They've got space between two exhibitions, so the event should be the following week. It's not that long. It's really not.'

I glanced across and saw her wince. She shook her head and breathed in sharply through her nostrils.

'Sarah! You know that you can't let the exhibition go ahead. This is all so wrong.'

I didn't speak. I just looked down at the footpath as we kept walking, the silence tense.

'Also, this really isn't fair on me,' Nel added, very quietly.

'I know it isn't fair on you. I'm so sorry, Nel. But I'm begging you. We've been friends since we were teenagers. You know I'm a good person. Please? Just give me time to sort things out. I promise that I will.'

I kicked a pebble, and it skidded down the dusty path.

'Well, how about you still tell James and both the boys?' Nel eventually suggested. 'They're your family. I'm sure they'll keep your secret safe and then at least they could stop worrying. I just can't imagine how they feel . . .'

Of course I didn't want to hurt my family. I could put a stop to all of it. It would only take a short phone call. But what exactly would I say? What could I say? The truth was just too awful.

'They would hate me, Nel,' I quietly said. I stopped walking and grabbed her hand. I squeezed it hard. 'They can't ever know I lied to them. They really can't. I'm the person they rely on, and to know that I'd betrayed that trust . . .' Panic flamed inside my rotten core. 'You promise that you'll never tell? You promise, Nel?'

Nel sighed and shook her head again.

'Of course I do,' she said, sounding resigned. 'But Sarah, please …'

'Two weeks. That's all! That's all I need.'

'Two weeks,' she repeated. She looked down at her feet and ground her sandalled toes into the path. 'Okay, two weeks. But you promise that you'll sort this out. It feels so wrong.' She paused, then said. 'It *is* so wrong.'

'Of course,' I said, my voice too high. 'You can trust me, Nel.'

She didn't respond. Had I lost my friend in all of this? Was the damage irreversible?

'So, are you ready for this lunch then?' she finally asked, sounding strained. 'The one with Lia.'

I was relieved she'd changed the subject and I gave a shaky laugh. 'Of course I'm not. I don't know what on earth to wear.'

Nel knew how bad I was at choosing clothes and how much time it took me to decide. I didn't own that many outfits that I genuinely liked, that were fashionable or fitted me. Yet despite the lack of options, on the rare occasions I went out, I'd somehow end up spending hours trying on the things I knew looked wrong. I would drag armfuls of ancient clothes from out the *Songesand* wardrobe and embrace them in my arms as if hugging all the previous iterations of myself. Versions that were younger, thinner, prettier or pregnant would end up flung across the double bed, abandoned in a growing pile.

We walked up the hill. Sweat was slowly dripping down my back and seeping from the places where my fleshy parts encountered other fleshy parts. I was soggy in the creases. Cupping my hand around the back of my neck, I felt my hair curling with damp. I stopped to catch my breath.

Nel turned and studied me, my hands on my knees as I bent over. 'Sarah, you know that all this lying isn't good for you. Or anyone. I'm not sure I've ever seen you look so tired.'

She hadn't meant this as a compliment but I remember feeling deeply pleased the moment that she said that. If I looked genuinely bad, then people would believe that I was ill. And the truth was that I *was* tired. Beyond tired. I was totally exhausted.

On the Saturday I woke early and went downstairs to carry on my research. I was googling medications used for breast cancer and I remember that the cat was sitting in the middle of the kitchen floor, its legs splayed wide, licking at its pale pink pinch of arsehole. Outside the sky was grey and dense. I clicked through numerous links written by charities, scoured pages from the NHS, downloaded PDFs from private hospitals, reading everything and anything I could. And that was when I found it. The details of a drug called

Cyclophosphamide Cytoxan. I whispered the medication's name, accentuating all the individual consonants, as if the words were brand new clothes that I was trying on for size. I moved my lips, added emphasis to the repeated 'o's, and said the words again until they started to sound natural, rolling easily from my tongue. I rubbed my palms together and felt something like excitement. I believed that things would be okay.

Cyclophosphamide was a treatment that could be administered in tablet form; I could medicate myself. This would make lying so much easier. I found the dosage details and used the calculator on my phone to estimate the dose I'd need if I really did have cancer. Taking a single tablet every day would be far easier than pretending to have IV drugs. I could simply buy a batch of multivitamins and pretend that they were medicine. The only thing I'd need to figure out now was a bottle that looked believable with a forged prescription label – which wouldn't be impossible for a person who could draw, who held an art degree from St Martin's.

Ryan walked into the kitchen as I was searching Amazon and Etsy for a small brown plastic bottle, one that resembled a chemist's bottle. Adrenalin surged through me and I snapped my laptop shut. The cat jumped up and hissed at me.

'You startled me,' I said. 'I didn't hear you coming in. How long have you been standing there?' My face burned red.

Ryan shrugged his skinny shoulders. 'Dunno,' he said. 'Not long,' he said. He didn't even look towards the laptop.

I watched him as he stood there. His long, stretched limbs and pale skin. A young man made of angles. Ryan was still growing at a frightening rate, and he looked gawkish and uneasy, as if he hadn't figured out how to inhabit his own body yet.

'Is everything okay?' I asked.

Ryan frowned, shifting his weight to lean against the doorframe, as if even standing upright was exhausting. He gnawed a fingernail. 'Yes,' he said. 'I'm going for a run. I really need to do some exercise. I need to get much fitter.'

He looked forlorn. As if the whole concept of exercise was entirely unappealing, a sentiment I fully shared.

'Fit-*ter*?' I asked, my eyebrows raised.

He smiled at that. 'Fine,' he said. 'Perhaps I'll start with getting fit.'

There was a twinkle in his eyes then. He came and draped his arms about my shoulders in a semi-awkward hug. He smelled slightly of cinnamon, of pungent weed and the inside of a hamster cage that was in desperate need of clean sawdust. I briefly cupped his face with both my hands. He closed his eyes and I marvelled at the miracle of his perfect feathered eyelashes, at this human that I'd birthed and grown. I brushed his fringe gently away and kissed him firmly on the forehead.

'Get off me, Mum,' he finally said, but the edges of his lips lifted into a smile and he didn't push me off. As he left, he told me that he loved me. Ryan had always been uncomfortable with expressing his own feelings and the words threw me, caught me off guard.

'I love you, too,' I said, but I could feel emotion clog my throat. My eyes burned, and I worried that I'd start to cry. For a second, I imagined the relief I'd feel if I just let the tears escape along with the dark truth. 'I'm not leaving you. I'm fit and well. I love you, son.' That's what I wanted to say. But if I told him he would hate me for the pain I'd caused. So instead, I shook my head.

'Enjoy your run,' I called after him as he walked away and down the narrow hallway. We both knew that he wouldn't.

That afternoon Bo took me out, insisting that she treated me. I kept saying no, I really tried, but my refusal was beginning to sound rude. I didn't want to offend Bo, which was how I ended up having my nails done.

I had never had my nails done professionally before. It had always seemed a waste of time, and an even greater waste of my small earnings. I'd never even bothered painting them myself. Given the amount of washing up I usually did, my nails were bound to flake and chip.

'But that's precisely why people get gels,' Bo said. 'They'll be fine for weeks,' she'd reassured and so I'd finally relented.

The nail salon was neat and clean, with tiles plastered on the walls and a row of large vibrating chairs, where women sat beside each other, their feet submerged in pools of soapy water. The atmosphere was friendly and every time the door opened a bell tinkled. One lady started giggling, her feet clearly too ticklish to be comfortably touched and she emitted yelps and high-pitched squeals which appeared to be contagious. Soon the entire room was grinning. All except a single woman seated near the back who had her eyes closed and her head tipped back, large headphones on, whilst her feet were being massaged soft with lotion. She looked so relaxed and so content and the place had felt so joyful that I began to wonder what I'd been missing out on for all these years.

Sitting at an individual table beside Bo, I was presented with a book full of bright colours. It looked a little like the box of watercolour paints that I used to use at art college, and I couldn't help but smile at the memory. I rubbed my fingers across the swabs as I scrutinised the different shades, each one denoted by a number. There were vibrant reds and garden greens, some urban greys and an entire page of pastel pinks. There were colours flecked with glitter, a metallic range that shimmered when you held them up into the light and a shiny gothic black. The brilliant white reminded me of painting all my nails with a small bottle of Tippex during double maths at secondary school, in an attempt to stave off the extreme boredom.

'Have you decided yet?' asked Bo, pointing at a florid shade of pink that she'd picked for herself.

'I'm not quite sure …' I fumbled, flicking through the many pages of the colour book. The choice was vast. I ran my fingers over russet browns and deep maroons. I loved them all. The lady to my left had chosen a bright red, the colour of a post-box, and I remember feeling tempted.

'I've an idea,' Bo said. 'Let's get the same!'

'I'm not sure that would suit me,' I said, looking again at the bright pink that she'd chosen. It reminded me of bubble gum. 'I think that I'm too old for that.'

Bo looked down sadly at her lap and quietly said, 'I would really love it if our nails matched. For me, Sarah?'

I had no idea how to say no. It also didn't help that she was paying for the manicure. So, I let the nail technician, with her face mask and her pretty eyes, paint my nails a vibrant shade of pink. A shade I never would have chosen. I barely knew who I'd become.

When I made it home later that afternoon, I found Ryan in the kitchen. His face was grim. He was sitting on a chair, holding a damp tea-towel that was twisted into a small sack. Lying on the table next to him there was a bag of ice cubes from the freezer. He pressed the cold compress against his ankle.

'Oh my God, what happened, Ryan?' I cried, rushing

towards him and crouching down to get a better look. The ankle was an angry red and swollen. A layer of sweat sprang out across my forehead, and I wiped it with my forearm, whilst trying not to panic. The run hadn't gone well, then.

The cat began to rub itself against my leg, its body pressed against my thigh. It probably wanted feeding. I nudged the cat away and it slunk into the garden through the cat flap, ignoring the back door which was wide open. I watched it sidle off into the shadows of the hedge.

'It's nothing, Mum,' Ryan said, avoiding any eye contact, moving his leg beneath the kitchen table, out of view.

I sighed. 'Ryan,' I tried again.

'Just stop,' he said.

He went to stand and immediately grimaced, clearly struck with pain. He began to limp towards the kitchen door, clutching the ice-filled tea-towel. I watched his painfully slow exit. The ice cubes had started melting, and as he walked away from me, a thin dribble of water trailed across the sparkling floor.

'Please let me look,' I pleaded.

'I said that it was nothing!' Ryan firmly said, his words clipped as he hobbled away.

But it clearly wasn't nothing. My son was in a lot of pain, and for the first time in his life, he wouldn't let me help him.

~

On Monday Lia, the owner of the gallery, arranged to meet me at a restaurant. The restaurant was glamourous, a famous institution that I'd only ever seen on Instagram, located in a smart side street in Marylebone. I arrived ten minutes early and the waiter sat me in a booth. I remember the dark leather seats, deep polished wood and the solid silver cutlery with their satisfying weight.

'Sarah!' Lia's voice trilled as she strode across the restaurant wearing a pair of open-backed high-heels and a shimmering black jumpsuit that I doubt she'd bought from H&M. The heels made a tapping noise which sounded like the pigeons nesting on our bedroom roof. 'It's so good to finally meet you,' she said smiling.

'You too,' I said.

I watched her face as she opened her large handbag and put her phone away. The woman could have been any age from thirty-five to fifty-five, depending on how close you were, the angle and the lighting. She tipped her dark sunglasses back onto her head, revealing vibrant hazel eyes, leaned her body towards mine to kiss the air.

'Sorry,' she said. 'I don't do physical contact. Thank God for all that Covid mess. At least it stopped people from shaking hands. Such an unhygienic habit.'

I quickly hid my hand back beneath the corner of the tablecloth.

'I live with men. It's probably for the best,' I said.

Lia pulled a face which made the skin around her nose ruche. Her forehead didn't crease and the skin around her eyes stayed firm.

'So,' she said, sliding herself into the padded booth across from me. She laid her linen jacket down on the leather bench and smoothed the creamy fabric with a hand. She gestured at the waiter, her nails neatly manicured. I was so grateful in that moment for my own bright nails. 'Still please,' she said.

We waited for the young man to fill our glasses before he slipped away to leave us with the menus. 'Well, first things first. Let's order food.' She turned her menu over and left it face down on the table, clearly so familiar with the place that she knew exactly what to have.

The menu looked delicious. Anchovies with orange zest. Small plates of Nocellara olives. A cuttlefish and wine ragu, and linguine cooked with salty clams. To finish, there was baked ricotta cheesecake and a range of sorbets and ice-creams. My mouth flooded at the promise of a creamy panna cotta drowning in a rich magenta berry sauce, that I'd seen leaving the kitchen.

'I'm going to have to restrain myself. I'll be eating lots of cake later.'

I explained that it was Bo's birthday and that we had a family dinner planned.

'Lovely,' Lia said distractedly, whilst examining the wine list, her face stiffened into a smile. She gestured to the waiter, and without asking what I preferred ordered us a bottle of Viognier, which cost more than my weekly shop.

Lia chose paella cooked with giant prawns still in their peony-pink shells and mussels that had cracked open like pavements in a heatwave. I was surprised she didn't want some sort of salad without dressing or at least a dish devoid of carbs. Instead, she took a fork, attacked the shells, and began spooning large heaps of steaming rice into her mouth.

'God, I love it here,' she said, dabbing at her lipstick with a crisp white linen napkin so bright and starched it looked brand new.

I loved it too. I twirled my fork around, collecting lengths of creamy pasta, whilst the waiter filled my wine glass. The wine was unlike anything I'd tried before. It smelled of swathes of breeze-blown fields, vanilla pods and lemon trees and it tasted of a different life. I loved everything about the place. The ambience. The perfectly laid tables. The glasses that were elegant and delicate. The warm bread rolls sprinkled with seeds. The butter, salty and unfathomably soft.

'We're so thrilled that you're exhibiting with us,' Lia said, pulling a prawn apart and sucking at her fingers one by one.

'I'm really glad too,' I said, my cheeks flushing with pride. 'And I'm so incredibly grateful. I want to thank you for the opportunity again.'

'Of course,' she said, waving my thanks away. 'Your work carries great emotional weight. I like the fact that images of ordinary domestic chores have been given added meaning as a consequence of your poor health.' I pinched my thigh beneath the table. 'How are you feeling by the way?' she asked, looking suddenly concerned.

I screwed my toes up in my shoes. 'I'm taking one day at a time,' I said, staring at a blank space on the table. I squeezed my thigh again, then squeezed it even harder. I pinched the flesh until it smarted like a fresh bee sting.

'That's exactly what we all should do,' she said, swiftly. 'We obviously want to hold the exhibition before you start treatment, which I imagine will be very soon.'

I nodded.

'I really shouldn't say this, but from a marketing per-spective, your situation is a PR dream. The cancer thing is clearly awful, but it will help you launch your art career. So,' she said, raising a glistening glass, 'here's to silver linings.'

We toasted and I took a swig of wine, drank it thirstily like water. The waiter appeared to refill my glass.

'What if I wasn't ill?' I asked, attempting to sound nonchalant.

'But you are, Sarah,' she said, as if the question were ri-diculous. 'You are gravely ill.' She placed a hand briefly on mine and then went back to breaking mussel shells apart.

'Just imagine for a second that I wasn't though,' I said, watching her eat.

Lia laughed at that, a confident and high-pitched laugh.

She stopped laughing abruptly when she saw the expression on my face and laid her fork down on the table.

'Oh, you're serious,' she said. She cocked her head to one side, clearly thinking. 'Well, if it wasn't for the angle – that you've made these drawings for your sons when faced with your mortality, and a future that's uncertain ...' She screwed up her nose. 'Umm ...' She wiped her fingers on the napkin, unfolded it, refolded it again. 'Your drawings would be lovely still – I mean, they're undeniably beautiful – but they wouldn't have the same appeal or hold the same commercial value.'

I placed my glass back on the table, set my face into a rigid smile. 'Well, I guess it's good I'm sick, then.'

If it were possible for her brow to crease, it would have then. I nervously laughed.

By the time we'd finished eating we'd agreed upon a date for the exhibition. I'd handed her the sketchbook and granted her permission to turn the drawings into signed, framed prints to be sold inside the gallery. My fingers lingered on the sketchbook, struggling to let it go. And then I did. It felt so strange to be parted, as if I'd lost an actual friend. I'd spent so many hours engaging with its contents, filling it with time and love, that giving it away to someone other than my sons felt uncomfortable and wrong. I should have listened to my feelings then. The work had been intended for my boys alone, not as a springboard for an art career. Why couldn't I have been content? Instead, I'd wanted even more. I couldn't see that what I had already was enough.

I wish I'd understood that then.

Before I ruined everything.

That evening we celebrated Bo's birthday. At least, we tried to celebrate. By the time I arrived home the sky was dark and ominous, the clouds heavy and low. I remember how the light changed in the kitchen, how it felt like night despite the early evening hour. I wiped my floury hands across my apron, put the cake tins in the dishwasher and opened the white wine that I'd forgotten to chill. Left out in the kitchen, it had warmed through like a can of Heinz tomato soup. I drank a large glass anyway, adding ice cubes from the freezer. I didn't care about the taste; I just wanted to switch my brain off.

'Bo's running late,' Olly announced, as he walked into the kitchen, pulling his wired ear buds out his ears, whilst simultaneously loosening his tie. Thunder rolled outside and fat raindrops began to spatter against the window-panes. Olly's hair was slick and his pale pink shirt was dotted with large, damp spots that made me think of gunshot wounds.

'How late?' I asked.

I pressed a freshly cut strawberry into the generous layer

of frosting. The idea that I'd be making a birthday cake for Bo would have been completely unimaginable just weeks ago. Now, I was baking for the woman who lived in my home, with her soft smooth skin and perfect face and youthful breasts that stayed exactly where they were without an underwired bra.

'Half an hour, tops. She's just finishing some work calls. There's a house on Eastern Road that's being sold next week at auction.'

Olly sounded reasonably excited, droning on about the wonders of the local housing market and the benefits of auction for securing a quick sale at a competitive price. Normally I would have moved the conversation onto something a little more exciting, but Olly had hardly said a word to me since my fake-cancer diagnosis.

'Hey, Dad,' he said, as James entered the kitchen, rubbing his freshly showered hair with the edges of a bath towel.

James looked even more exhausted than he usually did. His face was pale, his shoulders stooped. But then he worked so hard, and for long hours. The shadows etched beneath his eyes, that had darkened over the past few days, weren't caused by me. They couldn't be. Or at least that's what I told myself.

'Nice to see you too, stranger,' James said, smiling at Olly.

'Is Ryan here?' I asked. 'He's hurt his ankle pretty badly. He should be at home and resting.'

I noticed that the strawberries on the birthday cake were leaching blood-red juice into the frosting.

'He's not upstairs,' said James, shrugging. 'I think he must be out. Perhaps it wasn't all that bad?'

'It was,' I said whilst frowning.

Ryan had been limping when I'd left for lunch, still refusing an appointment with the doctor. I'd made him promise that he wouldn't run again whilst his ankle was still swollen. Had he lied to me when he'd agreed? I wondered why he'd do that?

Minutes later, we heard a door key in the lock and then the sound of trainers squeaking along the hallway floor. Ryan was mumbling underneath his breath, hissing with pain. When he limped into the kitchen, he looked like he'd been swimming, with the exception that he didn't stink of chlorine, the trademark scent of the local leisure centre. His hair was plastered to his skull and his tracksuit bottoms and T-shirt were so completely drenched they'd turned a darker shade of grey. The fabric clung onto his skin like wet concrete. He ran his fingers through his hair, scattering water droplets everywhere. Somehow, he looked both simultaneously flushed and very pale.

'I had to go running,' he puffed, by way of explanation. 'I'm raising money for Breast Cancer. I've already got a couple of sponsors.'

My stomach churned. I swallowed bile.

'*Oh God,*' I thought.

Ryan blinked the water from his eyes and I looked down at his ankle.

'And it's raining still,' he panted.

As if to emphasise the point, a violent roar of thunder travelled through the leaden air. It sounded like the sky was buckling, breaking underneath the weight of rain-drenched clouds. I waited until the rumbling stopped.

'I really don't think you should run,' I said.

'I'm fine,' he snapped.

'So, how far did you get?' asked Olly, clearly trying to break the tension. Ryan told us that he'd run around the boating lake, followed by a larger loop around the park and then down the hill towards the tube. James passed Ryan his towel and Ryan slumped at the table where he vigorously rubbed his hair, the friction turning into sound. The cat lay down in front of him and Ryan stroked the creature's back. It closed its eyes, its life simple and easy.

The rain started lashing at the windowpanes. There was a puddle on the ledge which had expanded, and the water started trickling down the paintwork. As I went to close the window, I noticed that the air smelled sweet, of hot tarmac and sodden soil and I vaguely recollected Donna telling me at work one day that the aroma had an actual name. I had looked it up: *petrichor.* I had made a random guess at the correct pronunciation and rolled the sound around my mouth.

It was caused by a reaction with the plant oils and bacteria found in soil, something I almost wished I didn't know.

When Bo got home from work the cake was waiting in the centre of the table, fresh strawberries piled on the top around a smattering of pink candles that matched our vibrant nails. The house smelled of vanilla, jam and rain-drenched grass and the table was already laid with plates and pretty tissue napkins that I'd curled inside the glasses. Balloons were tied in coloured clusters and hung from all the kitchen lights, thin ribbons snaking down in coils, and I'd propped her birthday cards on different surfaces around the room.

When my family were all seated at the table, I sunk a knife into the sponge and cut a generous slice for Bo. She had blown the birthday candles out, closing her eyes to make a secret wish that no one asked her to divulge. Thin smoke trails loitered in the air. This should have been a celebration, but nobody smiled.

'Happy birthday, babe! Here. Have some cake.' Olly handed Bo a generous slice.

She pushed the cake around the plate, dented the frosting with her fork prongs. I noticed there were dark smudges beneath her eyes that didn't seem to be mascara. Her forehead was creased, her eyebrows close.

'I'm fine,' she said, not looking fine. She laid down her fork. 'It's just that we can't eat this. I read online that sugar can fuel cancer cells and we're all here to support Sarah. So, none of us can eat the cake.'

'I'm pretty sure the sugar link is unproven,' I tried, my voice too high.

'And the cake, it isn't vegan. We all need to become vegan.'

James looked at me for help. I pulled a face.

'Well, how about some strawberries then?' James tried, sounding resigned. 'Or wine? I'm pretty sure that all white wine is vegan.'

His words were slow, the syllables too loose, the vowels elongated and lethargic. James looked tired and defeated as he poured more wine into his glass from the almost empty wine bottle. We all looked at Bo, and her plate of untouched cake and her pile of untouched strawberries. The strawberry juice was pooling again, resembling a small crime scene.

'No, thanks,' Bo said, avoiding eye contact with everyone.

'Are you sure that you're alright?' I asked.

Bo pushed her plate away from her and began to shake her head. Her hair drooped in strands around her face and I noticed that her chin was covered with a smattering of tiny spots.

'It's just not right. You being ill,' Bo said, her face red and her voice angry. 'It isn't fair.'

She began to cry. The salty tears left trails down her cheeks. 'It feels wrong to celebrate. If the treatment doesn't work, you might not even get to be here for my next birthday and you're the closest person to a mother that I have.'

The air caught in my healthy lungs.

Bo pressed her face into her palms, whilst Ryan and Olly grimaced.

'Bo, Sarah is tough. She'll be just fine,' James said, taking my hand, squeezing my fingers hard.

I could feel Bo's words filter through my bloodstream and finally settle in my heart, like a great weight.

'Oh Bo,' I said.

Her face looked pale and dismal. I had to put an end to things, for the sake of my whole family. But if I told them now, they'd hate me and I was terrified I'd lose them. I was already in too deep. Also, it wasn't very long before the exhibition would take place. Just eight more days. Eight meagre days. If I'd told my family I was well, then all the lying would have been for absolutely nothing. So, I let Bo cry. I let her cry believing she could lose me. I let my sons fear they could lose me too. I stared at my plate, wishing I could cram vanilla sponge into my lying mouth and suffocate my feelings.

I returned to work on Tuesday and found Casey in the kitchen. This was a moment I'd been dreading. Casey was the one who'd set the fundraiser up, which was making my artistic dreams come true and I was so grateful, but if she'd never got involved at all, I probably wouldn't have ever lied. A small part of me blamed Casey for the mess I'd made.

'Oh, it's so, so good to have you, back!' Casey exclaimed. Her Geordie accent made the sentence undulate, the rhythm bounce. I handed her a coffee mug, added a large, heaped spoon of sugar to my own. Sugar was even more appealing now that it was banned at home.

'Thank you,' I said, and I smiled at her tightly.

'You know,' she said, gripping her mug. 'This was never what I planned to do. I only took this job because I needed to. But because of you . . . Well, you should know that you're my hero.'

I was lost for words, unlike Casey.

'You're an incredible mum,' she generously said. 'And then you come to work, and you really make a difference in these people's lives. And you do it with humility and kindness. This job, it really means something. I admire you so much, Sarah. And I feel bad . . .'

'You do?' I asked. I swallowed hard.

'Of course I do! It shouldn't have taken a cancer diagnosis for me to tell you just how much I think of you. You genuinely mean the world . . .' She trailed off.

I gripped her hands and squeezed them hard, until I finally managed to say, 'Thank you'. My eyes pricked and I rubbed at them, smudging my poorly applied eyeliner.

'Here. Let me fix your make-up. Just look up,' she said,

taking mascara from her handbag and deftly touching up the lashes on the lower lids. She frowned in concentration, gently combing, then stood backwards to admire her work. 'All done!' she said.

I tried my very hardest not to cry. I'd had absolutely no idea that Casey felt that way. I'd imagined that she'd pitied me and saw me as a woman with no options. My life had always seemed so small and the work we did lacked glamour. I wondered if I'd got things wrong and perhaps my life wasn't that bad. But only for a brief moment.

As soon as Casey left me, I took out my phone. By this point I had become undeniably addicted to checking the JustGiving page. The amount being donated had now reached almost four thousand pounds. Not only did I find the figure totally astonishing, but the fact that all these people were donating money to raise the profile of my art was utterly remarkable. I couldn't quite believe it. I was a nobody, a normal mum, a woman who worked long hours as a carer and even longer unpaid hours inside the home. Yet, four thousand pounds suggested that I might be more. More than those very ordinary things. It implied that I had talent and a future as an artist. It suggested I was special. I said the word 'artist' aloud. I said it twice. It made me feel better about the lies I'd told, and I liked the way it sounded and how my tongue coiled around my mouth.

I was obviously going to give all of the money back.

I wasn't a total monster! After the exhibition I'd simply pretend that the hospital had made a huge mistake, and I would return all the donations. Every single last penny to every single person. It wasn't really stealing if I never planned to spend it. There would be absolutely no harm done, or so I let myself believe as I turned all my attention to the washing up. Surprisingly, I found that I quite missed it.

My family wouldn't let me clean a thing now, insisting that I rest instead and conserve my precious energy for the things I loved, but it felt so good to keep my hands busy and my mind occupied. I washed the coffee cups, then scoured the tiny kitchen, swept the biscuit crumbs into the bin, rearranged the chipped, mismatching mugs so that they lined up in a pleasing row and scrubbed the stainless-steel sink until it sparkled. The halogen glare refracted off the sink and made it shine like London streetlights in the winter. My breathing calmed, and I smiled as my heartbeat finally slowed.

'Sarah!' A woman's voice rang out, reprimanding and concerned. I turned to see my manager, Sue. She had found me rifling through the fridge, removing all the almost-empty cartons of long-ago expired milk. She wore a too-tight jacket and her short, cropped hair was bleached white blonde and sticking up at angles. It reminded me of freshly sprouted cress seedlings, like the ones the boys had grown in empty eggshells and brought back home from primary school to sit proudly on the windowsill. 'I know you want to be here, but someone else can do all this.'

Sue waved towards the clean kitchen, the kitchen I was proud of.

'I'm fine,' I tried. 'I promise. I'm not in need of special treatment.'

'I thought that you might say that. But please could you just humour me?' she said. The question sounded like an order. She clasped my shoulders and squeezed them hard. I could smell her coconut hair wax, and the faint aroma of tobacco mixed with petrol fumes from the Vesper that she rode to work.

'Don't make me pull the boss card!' she warned, smiling. 'We all just want to help somehow.'

I looked back towards the milk cartons that I'd planned to rinse and the recycling that needed sorting. It would have been so satisfying.

After Sue left, I took my sugared coffee and headed to the large and sunny day room. Casey was settled in the corner with a group of four, who were all huddled over paper, holding pencils.

'Legs Eleven!' Casey called, immediately followed by 'Snakes Alive!' Then someone shouted 'Bingo!' and the others groaned.

'You don't fancy playing Bingo?' I asked Donna, pulling out a chair to join her in the far corner.

Donna always made me feel better about life. I loved hearing her stories and the friendship that we had felt real. Now, she looked deep in thought, staring out of the window at the car park. She smoothed her skirt across her lap. It was the colour of fresh apricots, the pleats ironed and perfect. Despite the day's warmth, she wore a pair of flesh-toned tights and a pale cream blouse with a silver brooch in the shape of a horse chestnut leaf.

'No, not today,' she muttered without looking at me.

I began to feel uneasy as I took her crinkled hands in mine. They reminded me of the maps we used to make at school, the edges lightly ashed with curling lighter flames, the paper aged with wet tea bags. Her liver spots floated like little islands, the raised blue veins the ridges of a mountain range.

'Is there anything that I can do?' I asked, concerned.

'You're so kind, but no. I'm not sad, dear. Not sad, at all. I just don't think that I'll be here long.'

'Oh, Donna. No! Have you had bad news?'

My heart leapt up into my throat and it started pounding faster. This must have been exactly how my family felt, powerless and apprehensive. But I didn't think about that at the time. This was a taste of my own medicine that I completely failed to notice.

Donna gently laughed, patted my hand. I watched her eyes crease at the corners as her smile enveloped her whole face. 'The opposite in fact. My daughter up in Yorkshire . . .'

'Heather?' I asked, hungry for reassurance.

'Yes, Heather. Well, the company is doing well and so they're moving house. They've asked if I'd move in with them. There's a cottage in the garden and I could see more of the grandchildren.'

'Oh, thank God! You really scared me, then. That's wonderful! I'll miss you, but that's wonderful!'

Together, we gazed out at the car park as Donna told me all about the view she'd have from her new cottage when she moved there in the autumn. The field outside the window would be full of cows, their stomachs huge and swollen, as the trees across the valley flamed. The fallen leaves around the base of distant trees would form circular pools. Clay red and pumpkin orange, gold, fanning the grass in soggy piles. As she spoke my pulse began to slow. A man was struggling with the exit barrier, his head leaned far out of the window of his car, jabbing buttons with his fingers, clearly angry.

'And you, Sarah? How is everything with you?' Donna suddenly asked. She looked at me intently. 'You've been off work, and people here seem to think that you're unwell. They're wrong, of course. But you should tell them all what you told me. You should stop all of these rumours so that people can stop worrying.'

My face froze. I had no idea what I should say. I'd presumed the staff who worked with me would keep the things they thought they knew all to themselves. Sharing details of my health was unprofessional, and I doubted that the older people would have found out any other way. They didn't seem to spend a lot of time online and I'd been certain that Casey's Facebook post and news of the JustGiving page wouldn't ever reach them. But as I looked around the Day Centre, I noticed people staring. I'd got things wrong. So very wrong. Everyone, except Donna, now believed that I had breast cancer.

'I don't know what you mean,' I said quickly. 'Of course I'm sick.' I tried to keep my face still, my expression blank.

I watched Donna's forehead crease, and her lips seal tightly closed.

I stayed silent, steadfastly loyal to my lie and her expression quickly turned to hurt. There was an awful pause as I felt a chasm open up between us. I could see that Donna felt it too. Our friendship irrevocably cracked.

'But,' she tried, 'you told me that . . .' She looked so deeply wounded but in order to protect the lie, I would have to make this sacrifice. I would have to ruin our friendship.

I needed everyone to think that I was sick, or I'd risk losing my family. And my family, they were everything.

'I don't know what you're trying to say,' I said again, attempting to keep my voice light. Our eyes were locked.

Deep horror swirled inside me, as I told Donna that she'd got things wrong, that I'd never told her I was well.

'I may be old but I'm not senile,' she said, her face hardened against me.

I squeezed her hand, but she pulled away and turned her face towards the window. Then, I walked away and didn't look back. I was an awful, awful person.

On the Wednesday my shift didn't begin until the afternoon, and everyone was out of the house. I used the quiet hours of the morning to create a tablet bottle for the bogus medication that would treat my made-up illness. I had ordered a small bottle in an opaque brown from an Etsy shop online, and then I'd found an image on the Internet of a label for Cyclophosphamide Cytoxan. The whole thing would have been considerably easier if I'd been familiar with Photoshop, but I made do with my drawing skills and did my best to recreate the label, hand-tracing letters with a fine liner that was waterproof and didn't smudge. It took a few attempts to get the letters right and the result wasn't quite perfect but unless you looked too closely, it was hard to tell that the bottle was a counterfeit.

Pleased with the result I stashed the bottle in my handbag and stopped at the large Tesco on my way to work. I remember walking down the aisles, past the piles of fruit and vegetables, each item identical in shape and size, scrubbed free of earth. Everything seemed fake and cold. The lights shone bright. The aisles white. The aircon made me shiver, in my short-sleeved summer dress, as I supressed a yawn.

I'd hardly slept the night before and when I did, I dreamt that I'd come home from work to find James lying on the sofa with his legs up on a cushion and his shoes still on. A steaming mug of tea was balanced on the sofa arm beside him. I'd moved the tea onto the side table and noticed that the sofa had a brand-new wedding ring shaped stain. I rubbed and rubbed the fabric, but no matter just how hard I tried, the stain remained. The dream had left me feeling anxious and unsettled, although I couldn't fully articulate why.

That morning I'd decided that the best and only thing to do was to keep going. I didn't think I had a choice. I was already in too deep and the only way that I could see was down and through. I just needed to stay focused. I was still convinced I had control and that soon this would be over.

And so, I found myself standing in the aisle of multivitamins and minerals, scanning the many offerings as I tried to choose some tablets that would be my pretend chemo. The amount was overwhelming. There seemed to be a vitamin for almost every letter of the alphabet, each with strange-sounding names. Potassium, selenium, ashwagandha, chromium and zinc. I picked up a small bottle of Vitamin B6 and was shaking it against my ear, attempting to approximate the size of the individual tablets from the resulting sound, when a voice stopped me.

'Sarah?'

I recognised it instantly. The gentle sing-song rhythm and the subtle lilt. I spun around.

'I thought that it was you!' the woman said, her face brightening.

Casey stood in front of me, a bag of cheese and onion crisps and a chicken salad sandwich in the shopping basket looped over her arm.

'It is,' I said. 'It's me.' I forced a smile.

A mother with a tiny brand-new baby coiled inside a fabric sling and strapped tightly onto her chest came to stand beside us. 'Excuse me,' the woman said as she reached across and grabbed a jar of multivitamins that were supposed to help with hair loss. I smiled at her, recognising her exhaustion, but her eyes were glazed and she didn't seem to notice me, or anything around her.

'I like your nails,' Casey said, as the woman moved away.

I glanced down at my bright pink nails, noticing the way the light caught on their polished curves.

'I've been meaning to say thank you,' I stammered. 'For setting up the fundraiser. People have been so very generous.'

'It's the least that I could do,' she said. 'Isn't the power of the internet amazing? All that money that we've raised! Oh, are those for you?' Casey asked, noticing the bottle I was clutching in my clammy hands.

I nodded.

'Oh, let me buy them for you, please. I've been wanting to get you something tangible since you received your diagnosis. I thought about nice flowers, but they don't last for long. They always look so pretty for the first few days and then they wilt and die.' She flushed bright red, clamped a hand across her open mouth. 'Oh, Sarah, I didn't mean to say that word. I'm so unbelievably thoughtless. God!'

'It's fine,' I said, although the moment felt so awkward that a part of me was wishing that I could die right then and there.

'And the JustGiving page was just the start. I have a whole thing planned for you, but that's a big surprise. You'll find out very, very soon,' she said.

Casey grinned, which made my stomach sink further as I wondered what on earth she had in mind. I was hoping that she'd simply rounded up my favourite people from the Day Centre and organised some sort of card, or perhaps even some biscuits, especially now I couldn't eat sugar at home.

'But I'd also love to get you something really useful. Do those vitamins you're holding help you fight cancer? Please, I'll get them for you, Sarah. I insist.' She took the vitamins from me, without waiting for an answer.

'You can't,' I tried.

'I can!' she said, 'Are these meant to help if you have breast cancer?'

'I think so, yes,' I finally said.

'Great,' she said as she put her basket on the floor. 'Hang on a sec.'

I watched as she retrieved her phone from her back pocket and began to google supplements. Her forehead creased as she skimmed through digital pages, grabbing different bottles off the shelves, reading out loud, until her shopping basket was piled high with vitamins and minerals.

'Casey. You can't! That will cost you a whole week's wages.'

'It's fine,' she said, 'You're worth it.'

And so, the awful truth is that I let her spend her money trying to cure me of an illness that I didn't have.

Casey was going back to work after her lunch break and so we headed there together. The afternoon at work played out as normal – or as normal as it could be. I made endless cups of milky tea, helped the ladies to the toilet, combed the wispy threads of Frankie's hair so that it looked exactly how she always liked it. When Terrence spilled his mushroom soup down his short-sleeved shirt, I mopped him up.

But Casey kept checking up on me and fussing, asking if I wanted snacks, or needed extra rest breaks. I wished she'd simply let me be. I wanted a few hours where I could forget about the things I'd done and just get on. Work had always felt like an escape, at least for a few precious hours. It was a bonus that they paid me. But now, my issues infiltrated work and home. It seemed that my imaginary illness had spread, aggressively, like cancer, and was now affecting all the aspects of my life.

At some point in the afternoon Casey came into the kitchen where I was happily engrossed in adding spoons of bright white sugar to a cup of tea. She took my hand and dragged me out into the main dayroom where the older people were all waiting, and the staff were standing in a huddle to the side. It felt like someone's birthday, except that everyone was staring right at me, just me, and Sue was in the centre of the room clearly waiting for a silence to descend. Beside her stood a scrawny man, looking earnest and intent. I guessed that he was somewhere in his thirties, and his clothes looked oversized, as if they weren't actually his own.

The instant there was quiet Sue began to talk.

'So, we all know that Sarah is the very, very best of us.' Sue paused as cheers went up around the room. Terrence, who was sitting in the corner, with a tartan patterned blanket draped across his lap and a crossword on the table, wolf-whistled and winked at me. Even from a distance I could see the ochre-coloured stain spread down his front, from where he'd spilled his lunch. Sue ran her fingers through her cropped and spikey hair and waited for the clapping to subside. 'You're all aware by now that Sarah isn't very well.'

My stomach sunk into my pelvis. 'Most of you have seen the Facebook post or been sent the details of the JustGiving page. Thanks, by the way, to all of you who've spread the word and those who have donated.' I glanced around the room at all the open, smiling faces and Casey who was beaming. I wished that Sue would stop talking immediately. She carried on. 'So, us lot who have the privilege of working here have been trying to think of ways to help with Sarah's fundraising.'

I thought that I might vomit then. I could feel the bile filling my mouth, flooding the space around my tonsils. I swallowed the acrid bitterness. Across the room, I spotted Donna. She was watching me intently, her brow creased and eyes like darts.

'*Oh God,*' I thought.

Sue was still talking. 'So, this afternoon we have a very special guest. This gentleman is called George Behrman. He's a journalist from the *Ham and High*, and he's visiting us all today to interview Sarah.' She cast me a proud glance. 'It seems that she has talents that extend beyond the amazing work she does with us and it's time that everybody knew.'

My face felt hot. I was suddenly aware that I was existing

on a planet, rotating at a frightening speed around a giant burning sun.

'Oh God,' I said, out loud this time.

All the residents began to clap. All except for Donna, her eyes on fire as she scowled at me. Her lips had all but disappeared. I turned away and looked towards the journalist and Sue.

I know I should have walked out then. I know I should have done something. But I couldn't think of an excuse. I couldn't think of what to say to extricate myself, to release me from this moment I'd created.

The Day Centre felt suddenly hot. My trousers clung like bandages against my thighs. I found myself being steered towards a chair and I obediently sat down. George Behrman settled himself in front of me.

'Would it be okay to voice record the interview?' he politely asked.

I nodded, and as he fiddled with his mobile phone, I noticed that he'd bitten all his fingernails down to the quick. His fingertips looked pink and raw, and the cuticles had frayed like ripping fabric.

George Behrman pressed record and I clasped my hands together in my lap. I could hear my heartbeat clamour in my chest, as adrenalin swelled through me.

What if I messed my answers up? What if I gave myself away? What if he guessed my inner thoughts and somehow knew that I was lying? It was hard to fathom how one lie had spiralled into all of this. The lie was only ever for my family. I had planned to keep it so contained. And now here I was, sat with an audience and a journalist about to interview me.

The first question that he asked was how I'd fallen in love with drawing. A memory dragged itself up through the years. I was very small, cross-legged, sitting on the floor beside Mum's favourite chair. I could almost feel the woollen tights against my skin that made me itch and I swear had no elastic in. Mum had given me some paper and a pencil. I sketched the things surrounding me – my mother's feet, the table legs, the pile of magazines left on the floor. I remember feeling so content with a pencil clasped inside my tiny hand, my mother sat beside me.

I stuttered as I nervously recalled the scene, but the more I spoke, the easier speaking became. The audience sat in silence, other than the occasional sniff or muffled cough. For the first time in my life, I felt as though my story was important, as though I had something of value to say. Everyone looked interested. Everyone was listening.

When George asked me about art college, I couldn't help but smile as I remembered meeting Nel all those years ago in London and the nights we spent at Bagley's, long before the place was knocked down and replaced with fancy restaurants and architect-designed apartments that only bankers could afford.

I started telling stories of the projects that we'd worked on, and my deep love of illustration. As the minutes passed, I found that I was no longer feeling nervous. In fact, I'd go so far as saying that I was actually having quite a lot of fun. I was enjoying the attention whilst the conversation focused on my drawing skills. George Behrman continued asking questions and I answered every single one.

When the conversation inevitably turned to cancer I felt considerably less comfortable. I was terrified of messing up and outing my own secret.

'So, could you share your path to diagnosis? Were there signs or symptoms that you'd like to share?'

I scratched the inside of my wrist and avoided making eye contact.

'You can take your time,' he softly said. 'I can't imagine this is easy.'

I stopped scratching, took a deep breath and tried to only talk about the things that were entirely true. I recalled the horror of discovering a breast lump as I went to take a shower on the night before my birthday and the anxiety I felt when the GP referred me to the hospital.

I spoke about how the breast lump had inspired me to create an illustrated Life Guide for my sons, which was soon to be a gallery show and hopefully a published book.

'And how did you feel when you got the final diagnosis?

When they told you it was breast cancer?' George gently pushed.

I looked around the room at all the waiting faces. Casey caught my eye and softly smiled.

'It's hard to find the words,' I finally said.

Because the truth is that it really was.

George switched off the recording device on his mobile phone. Then he shook my hand.

'Thank you for all your precious time,' he solemnly said. 'Your story is really inspirational – the way you've used your trauma to inspire your art – and you've been an excellent interviewee. You've made my job incredibly easy.'

I nodded at him weakly.

'So just to let you know, the piece will probably run on Friday.'

'Great,' I said, my voice high-pitched.

'And for what it's worth, I love your work. The illustrations that I've seen are really very beautiful.'

My healthy chest swelled instantly with pride and I smiled at that. The lying was truly awful, but this part was something I could get used to, the praise and validation from a stranger. Just as I thought that it was over and that George would leave, Sue clapped her hands together. Silence spread across the older people, like a blanket.

'There's one last thing,' Sue announced. She paused as

George hastily unlocked his phone and began to voice record again. 'You've started having chemo,' Sue looked at me with pity. 'We want you to know that you're not alone. We're all here for you! And to show you that we mean it, Casey and I have both agreed to shave our heads.'

The whole room cheered.

For a moment, I was worried I'd stop breathing.

I quickly glanced at Donna. She just shook her head. I looked away.

It all happened very quickly. Someone pulled another plastic chair into the centre of the Day Room and a pair of clippers suddenly appeared. I pressed my nails into my thigh and wished that it would hurt more. I was living through a nightmare. A nightmare that was all my fault and one I wouldn't wake up from. Casey was now seated, a sheet wrapped round her shoulders like some sort of shroud, and Sue was holding up the clippers like a guillotine or heavy axe.

'Any final words?' Sue asked, as the journalist George Behrman held his phone closer to Casey.

There was a ringing in my ears that reminded me of church bells at a funeral.

'But what about auditions?' I squeaked. 'Don't you have another audition coming up this week?'

'Oh, I just won't go. I doubt I'd get it anyway and this is so much more important.'

Casey smiled then. A huge, wide smile. She tugged her hair-tie with her hand and her deep brown hair cascaded from her ponytail, voluminous and lovely, falling far below her shoulders. She was still beaming as she reached a hand up to her head and swallowed hard, patting with her fingers at her length of hair. The entire room was silent, still.

Casey gave a slow nod, and Sue nodded back as she switched the clippers on. The noise was like a swarm of bees, their hive disturbed, their bodies small and angry. My lungs struggled to draw in any oxygen. I willed the world to fade away. I closed my eyes and scrunched them tight. I listened to the buzzing sound and as Casey's hair fell to the floor, I swear it sounded like a secret being whispered.

Bo and Olly were both at home when I got back. Bo looked pale and tired, and she and Olly kept on muttering, their voices hushed, their words sharpened and angry, like tiny metal filings.

'What's wrong with Bo?'

I'd followed Olly out into the front garden. The glare was bright, and I squinted in the early evening light.

'She's fine. We're fine. Why wouldn't we be?'

Olly said the words abruptly as he was dragging the recycling out aggressively towards the curb. It was hard to properly hear him speak. Not only were the numerous empty wine bottles that filled the bin all clinking, rattling loudly, but a local council tree surgeon was busy amputating branches from the large plane trees outside the house, whilst suspended in the air waving a chainsaw.

'It's a health hazard,' yelled the tree surgeon, when he saw that I was staring.

The stumps looked strange, the trees naked without their smaller branches and dense covering of summer leaves. The air was full of fine sawdust. It gritted both our eyes and flecked our clothes, and I remember thinking that it felt intensely violent and somehow sad.

'Are you sure that Bo's okay?' I asked Olly, as I followed him into the house and closed the door behind us.

'It's just a stupid argument. Please leave it, Mum,' Olly said, and so I did leave it. It's awful but I felt relieved, more than willing to believe that at least this was a problem that wasn't caused by me.

The house smelled strangely empty. When Ryan wasn't out running, the smell of weed had become a constant once again. Great smoggy plumes. Acrid dense fumes, that streamed from the gap beneath his bedroom door. But at that moment the only thing I smelled was the fake pine scent of floor cleaner and the burning tang of toilet bleach.

'How was your run?' I asked Ryan when he eventually appeared at home.

Ryan slowly limped into the kitchen and headed straight

towards the sparkling sink. He stood facing away from me and filled a pint glass full of water. He downed the lot, and it made a glugging noise as the water travelled down his throat. I couldn't help but notice that the glass was shaking very slightly, a slight tremor travelling through his hands.

'How's your ankle? Are you sure it's strong enough to run on now?' I tried again, unsure if he had heard me.

He was steeped in sweat, which was pouring off his skin and soaking through his running clothes.

'Here,' I said, pulling out a chair, tapping the seat. 'Have you eaten anything today?' Ryan raised his shoulders slightly and slumped down at the table with his empty glass. My stomach clenched and tightened as maternal worry twisted through my bowels. I headed towards the cupboard, took a white Ikea soup bowl, a pint of milk from out the fridge and the large box of Rice Krispies. Ryan didn't move. 'Eat this,' I tried again, pouring a generous bowl and holding out a spoon. All I wanted in that moment was to mother him.

Ryan took the spoon and stirred the bowl of cereal as if it were cement that needed to be kept constantly in motion to stop it from setting firm.

'How are you, love?' I asked.

He made a strangled 'humphing' sound.

'That good?'

Ryan shrugged again. He began to prod and poke the

floating Rice Krispies, forcing them beneath the milk. They rose back to the surface. Pale maggots in an opaque pool.

'I'm really sorry, Ryan.'

I said the words sincerely. An apology for what I'd done. For how Ryan was feeling. For absolutely everything.

'It's fine. I'm absolutely fine,' he firmly said, pushing the bowl of cereal away, as if its presence was repulsive. He sounded a long way from fine.

I looked at him. His face had lost its ghostly sheen, all the time spent outside running exposing him to sunlight and fresh air but despite the subtle suntan, he looked far from well. Ryan dumped the cereal into the sink, took the stainless-steel strainer and threw the soggy waste into the bin, before wiping down the surface with a clean dishcloth. I should have felt elated that my son was finally cleaning up after himself, but I felt hollow and empty.

'You really don't look fine, Ryan,' I said, concerned.

'I'm fine,' he said more firmly. 'It's you we need to worry about. Not me.'

I chewed the inside of my cheek, a part of me he couldn't see. My son was running far too much, and I wondered if the thing that he was running from was actually me.

That night I went to bed early but couldn't sleep. When James came up much later, he found me lying in the semi-darkness, my face inches from my phone.

'You're not asleep?' He leaned over to kiss me. His breath was hot and vinegary, smelling strongly of white wine.

'I tried,' I said. 'I just feel so awful that Sue and Casey shaved their heads for me. I really wish they hadn't done that.'

'But why?' he asked, looking confused. 'They both wanted to, and I think it's really brilliant that you won't feel so alone when your own hair . . .'

I raised a hand to touch my hair and must have looked appalled because James temporarily stopped talking.

'I'm so sorry, love,' he tried again. 'I can't imagine what you're feeling right now.'

And he was right. He couldn't possibly comprehend the awful guilt that was threatening to engulf me as I smiled at him weakly.

James went to clean his teeth and I returned to staring at my phone. I'd spent the past few hours constantly refreshing the JustGiving page. It was hard to drag myself away. The total had now reached over five thousand pounds, and the amount was quickly climbing. The article in the *Ham and High* would likely push the number even higher and I wondered just how much I'd raise by the time that this was over. I was going to give all of the money back, but the fact that I had raised it in the first place still felt like validation. I tried to focus on the good feelings, on the sense of pride I felt. I did my best to push the memories of the day away.

I listened to James in the bathroom down the hallway. I heard the gentle running of the tap, the brushing of his toothbrush and the familiar sound his pee made as it hit the inside of the toilet bowl, the stream far weaker and less constant than it used to be. When he climbed back into bed, I reluctantly put my phone away and we lay together, both staring at the ceiling in the semi-gloom.

'I've been thinking, love,' he said finally. 'We haven't had a chance to talk, at least not properly, since you got home from the hospital. I want to know what I can do and what you need. Whatever it is. Just say, Sarah. I can take time off. I can work less hours. And I'll be there for appointments. I know I'm not too good at hospitals and I haven't been that great over the years at doing the domestic stuff, but I'm trying, and I'll make sure that I do better . . .'

'James . . .' I said, wanting desperately to reassure him, or at the very least to make him stop, but I didn't know quite what to say. 'I'm just so unbelievably sorry,' I eventually muttered.

'No!' he said, pushing himself onto his elbows.

James leaned across and switched on the beside lamp. Its soft glow filled the room and the furniture cast long shadows. He shook his head. 'Don't say that, please. You have absolutely nothing to be sorry for. I don't want to hear you say sorry ever again. You can't help the situation that you're in. Being ill isn't your fault in any way.'

I heard the last few words catch in his throat, the scratch of trapped emotion. I swallowed hard, felt sick inside.

'I love you, James,' I meekly said. I reached towards my husband and held my palm against his stubbly cheek. As a single tear escaped him and trailed down his cheek I rubbed it away, desperate to erase everything it symbolised, and all the dreadful things I'd done.

On the Thursday, I went back to work. Ever since I'd first met Sue, she had always had her hair cut short, the sides cropped close and the top spiked, aiming for a look that was androgenous and slightly punk. The new close shave didn't look too shockingly different. In fact, it almost looked intentional – especially with Sue's leather jacket, denim jeans and heavy boots. It helped that her face was naturally round, so that even with no hair she still looked healthy.

Whereas Casey just looked awful. Her slim young face was far too sharp to have no hair to frame it and her cheekbones were now too pronounced. Her skull wasn't as smooth as Sue's, with irregular dents and ridges. I found it hard to look at her.

I tried to avoid Casey, but the harder that I tried, the more often Casey appeared beside me like a mutilated shadow. I felt haunted by her hairless head, the skin too taut and shiny.

Usually, I'd spend my work breaks in the kitchen, chatting with a cup of tea to whomever happened to be there. Today, I went and sat outside on the bench that faced the car park and was originally used by staff who smoked, before smoking on the premises was banned.

I looked across the concrete, towards the scrappy length of hedge and at the flats that rose beyond. The balconies all revealed details about the people who were living inside. Some were jungle green with plants, others adorned with laundry. A balcony on the top floor was crammed full of junk. There was a child's bike, old boxes and a plastic Christmas tree that was still hung with silver baubles, glistening in the summer sun. When I blurred my eyes, the balconies resembled small, embroidered patchwork squares. The quilted fabric of other people's lives.

I only had a few moments before Casey came and sank down on the wooden bench beside me.

'I'm really worried about Donna,' she blurted out. Her eyes looked huge without her hair. There were pimples on her exposed skull.

'What do you mean?' My body tensed and I clasped my hands in front of me as I looked away.

'It's just, well, Donna told me that she thought I'd be so happy that tomorrow was the weekend.' Casey paused somewhat dramatically. I wondered what it was that I was meant to say.

'But today is only *Thursday*,' she said with added emphasis.

I paused, and then I laughed out loud.

'Oh,' I said, feeling relieved. I unclenched my hands and pressed my palms into my thighs, stretching my fingers wide and open. 'It's easy to get the days confused. Especially when you spend all of your days here. I really wouldn't worry.'

'It's not just that ...' Casey took a breath. 'I genuinely think there might be something wrong. She keeps on telling me you were given the all-clear, and that you told her you don't have breast cancer and that you never did. She even told me you were lying to the rest of us.'

'Oh God,' I said.

This was becoming a living nightmare. The only thing that I was grateful for was that Donna hadn't said something whilst the journalist was interviewing me. But I had no idea who else she might have spoken to. And what if somebody believed her?

'Oh God,' I said, a little louder.

'I know!' she said. 'I thought that I should let you know in case she brings it up with you. I thought that you should be prepared. I feel really sorry for her. I think she's probably far too fond of you to face the truth about your illness. Or she's becoming seriously confused. But either way, it looks like Donna's quite unwell.'

My stomach clenched. I swallowed bile. 'Hang on a bit. Let's not jump to any conclusions. I mean, it sounds as if she's got things in a muddle. But that doesn't mean it's serious.'

Casey pressed her lips together and shook her bald head. 'No. You honestly should have been there. Donna's adamant, and she seemed incredibly angry. The poor, poor thing.'

'Well . . .' I said, drawing out the word, trying desperately to formulate some sort of plan to protect both Donna and my lie, whilst simultaneously trying not to vomit. 'Can we keep this to ourselves?' I asked. 'At least, for now? If she says anything else that seems concerning, we can take it up with Sue. But until then . . .'

'Oh, I've told Sue everything already,' Casey said.

'You have?' I asked.

'Yes, I figured it was urgent. I know that Donna was planning to move up North to where her daughter is. But if this is the beginnings of dementia, and it looks as if it is, then she's going to need considerably more help. She can't be living in a cottage on her own. And I doubt her family have the time to properly care for her.' Her face relaxed. 'But, you don't need to worry about it. Sue's already called her daughter.'

The air left me. I think I groaned. I stared at all the balconies opposite, wishing that I lived somebody else's life. I would have happily swapped with any of the people living in those flats, even the person with the balcony stuffed full of junk. There was no way on earth that their life could be as messy and as complex as I'd made my own.

The day didn't get any better. Later that afternoon, Sue took me to one side to have a chat. She got straight to the point.

'Have you seen a surgeon yet?' she asked. 'Or is that all happening tomorrow?'

I'd told everyone that tomorrow was the day that I had to go back to the hospital again. I didn't want to take time off, to leave my colleagues understaffed and with more work, and to take sick pay when I wasn't actually sick at all, but everyone was expecting me to have appointments.

I tried to make myself feel better by telling myself that it would just be two appointments – one before the gallery show and a second shortly afterwards where I would pretend to get the shocking news that the hospital had messed things up. I would find out that I wasn't ill.

'Oh, I don't think I'll need a surgeon. I'll probably just need chemo.' I smiled and did my best to make the situation sound as unserious as breast cancer could be.

Sue's eyebrows knitted tightly. 'Really?' she asked. You're sure?'

I had an awful feeling there was only one right answer to her question.

'Pretty sure,' I nervously croaked.

Sue's eyes widened. 'So, is it metastatic cancer? Is it

terminal? Oh God, Sarah! I had no idea things were that bad.'

'No, it's not that bad,' I tried to reassure her.

She seemed confused and brought a hand up to the back of her head. Her elbow stuck out at a right angle. 'It's just my sister is a breast surgeon in Edinburgh, and our mum had breast cancer when the two of us were kids. It's probably why we do the jobs we do. It made us want to care for people.' Her mouth thinned. 'Most breast cancers require surgery. I think it's only four per cent of women who don't have surgery of some kind, and they're the tragically unlucky ones. I had no idea ...'

'Noooo,' I said, shaking my head. 'In that case I must be confused.' Sue bit her lip. My brain was scrolling fast as I tried to undo my mistake. 'It was hard to remember all the details,' I stammered. 'There was so much information to take in. I can't recall exactly what the doctor said. I must have that wrong. I'll definitely need surgery.'

I was panicking but the tension in Sue's face melted. She lowered her hand finally and smiled.

'I'm not surprised. Sometimes the doctors will use chemo first, to shrink the lump before they operate. Perhaps that's what they said to you?'

'Yes,' I said, 'that's what they said. I remember now. We're going to start with chemo.'

~

Arriving home, I was greeted with the stench of weed wafting out of an open window and a package on the doorstep. A neighbour down at seventy-two, a pregnant mother who already had a toddler, had left me a selection of new magazines as well as a handwritten note to tell me I was in her prayers. The only magazines I'd had the time to read in almost twenty years were the old ones at the dentist.

I took the pile of magazines out into the garden and sat down on the narrow concrete back doorstep. I breathed in the London air, the scents of petrol and parched summer grass. The step felt warm beneath my thighs. The garden wasn't very large, and it had been unloved for years. When the boys were small, I'd planted rows of bright sweet peas, dense patches of thin runner beans and towering clusters of sunflowers. Now, the grass was mainly clover with large patches of dust from where the boys had practised endless football shots, aiming at the battered wooden shed.

The cat had followed me outside and was soon caught up in a game of catching bees. It flattened itself in the grass, a terrible attempt at feline camouflage. Then it made a sudden leap, ungracious and embarrassing. In a leisurely manner, the bee moved out of reach, before settling on a nearby bush of lavender. I was certain that I'd heard somewhere that bees broke the laws of physics, their bodies supposedly too large to fly. Nel would definitely know the answer but I didn't feel as if I could call.

Abandoning the magazines, I began to google facts on bees and, apparently, I had things wrong. I learned that the specific angle of their wings creates a tiny local hurricane, which lifts the bee into the air.

*We're similar* I suddenly thought. We both contain the power to create a vortex of our own. A precise and perfect chaos that no one else can clearly see.

I was lost in thought when I heard the rattling of the front door. There was an intermittent banging sound, the scrape of metal against metal. My heart thudded. Was someone attempting to break in?

I got up and tiptoed down the hallway and crept towards the front bay window to peer out from behind the curtains. My phone was gripped in my damp hand, my finger poised above the number nine as I made out a silhouette on the front step. I let out an elongated sigh and went to open the front door.

'Olly!' I cried. 'You scared me then! Did you forget your keys again?'

Olly was swaying violently. He seemed to be attempting to stay upright, as if the ground beneath his feet had turned to water. A personal and unpredictable sea, with gigantic waves and wild tides.

'Thanks, Mum,' he slurred, as he pushed past me into the hall.

The words lacked density and structure and sounded far

too baggy as they left his mouth, like an ancient bra that had lost all its elastic. His eyes were red, his tie loosened to form a noose.

'What are you doing home?' I asked.

'We all went to the pub for lunch,' Olly mumbled as he leaned against the banister and tried to wrestle with his shiny shoes. The sea beneath his feet was clearly raging and he lost his balance suddenly, falling backwards, up against the stairs, landing firmly on his backside. The sound must have been loud enough to reach Ryan in his bedroom, to filter through the headphones of his PlayStation.

'Mum? Are you okay?' Ryan called down, appearing on the landing above us in a fug of smoke.

'I'm fine. It's fine,' I said, 'Your brother's home. He's just had a bit too much to drink, that's all.'

'I'm good,' said Olly angrily, as he tried and failed to get back up.

'For fuck's sake, mate,' Ryan said, as he limped downstairs to help, reaching out to grab his brother's flailing hand.

The instant that Olly managed to clamber to his feet and was balanced vaguely upright, he shoved his hands into his brother's chest, causing Ryan to stumble to one side. Ryan's ribs hit the curved edge of the banister and made a horrid thud.

'What the hell?' Ryan yelled, rubbing his side. He pulled himself back up to standing and turned to face his brother.

I remember looking at my boys. Their eyes were dark, their nostrils flared and I could hear their ragged breathing. They looked incensed. Wild. Intense.

'Just stop!' I cried. 'Stop all of this.'

But they were locked too deep inside their fury. Ryan was thin and far less physically strong, and also clearly very high, but the fact he hadn't been drinking gave him a significant advantage. Olly was angry, unpredictable and drunk. I stepped towards the raging pair.

'Enough!' I yelled. 'I really don't need *this* right now.'

The boys were wrapped around each other now in a violent embrace, and they moved as one. A human form with four elbows and a multitude of moving limbs that was set on doing damage.

'Just stop,' I yelled. 'Stop all of this.'

They didn't stop.

'I have cancer!' I shouted suddenly in desperation.

Immediately, I pressed my hand over my mouth, completely horrified by what I'd said. But those three words, those untrue words, they instantly worked.

The boys froze and then released each other slowly, unpeeling limbs and becoming separate people once again. They both stared sullenly at the floor, Olly swaying still, the only sound their fractured breathing. I wasn't sure what I should say. I realised then that my lie was a weapon with unthinkable force, and that I was wielding it with abandon.

I was losing control. The boys had never fought like this before, and I wondered if the stress of my pretend illness was the reason they were fighting. My heart ached. I was hurting all the people that I loved.

'I'm sorry, Mum.' Ryan spoke first, his head hanging like a toddler on the naughty step.

'I'm sorry, too,' Olly finally said, beneath his breath, before he turned and staggered up the stairs.

I had horrified myself. I needed to escape the confines of the house. The boys were both locked in their rooms; they wouldn't even miss me.

I thought a walk around the park might make me feel better, so I was waiting in the ice-cream queue at the kiosk when Lia called. The boy in front, who was only four or five, asked for 'a bubble gum' and was presented with a giant cone filled with a scoop of bright blue ice-cream. The ice-cream looked as far from edible as possible, almost poisonous. It was the same shade as the little blocks of chemicals that you place inside the cistern of the toilet to kill the germs and mask the stinging stench of male pee.

The boy began to take large greedy licks and soon his mouth was stained a dusky blue. His small, bowed lips looked drained of blood and despite the heat I shuddered, turned myself away.

The phone's ring startled me and when I saw that it was Lia, I quickly left the queue to answer it.

'How is everything?' Lia's voice cooed. She sounded like brushed velvet, or the inside of a creamy, hot, baked Camembert. 'So,' she said, before I'd had chance to say a word, 'I have something to ask you.'

I walked past a group of birds that had congregated around an overflowing bin. A collection of dark, mangy coots, some pigeons and a pair of female ducks, their feathers brown and drab. The birds hoovered the concrete hungrily and I felt guilty that I wasn't offering thick crusts of wholemeal bread or the bird food that they sold inside the park café and which ironically cost more than a hoisin-flavoured duck wrap bought from Sainsbury's.

'Oh yes?' I said, trying hard to hide the anxiety I felt. The entire situation felt like a bubble that could burst at any moment. The exhibition was a dream come true, but every other aspect of my life was feeling very far from dreamlike, and I was fearful that if the exhibition didn't take place, then the lying and the pain I'd caused would have been for absolutely no reason.

'So, how exactly would you feel about selling the originals?'

'Umm . . .' I said, slowing my pace. 'Well, I'd planned to give them to the boys when you'd finished making prints of them. I mean, the drawings were all meant for them.'

I stopped walking.

'Yes, that's obviously lovely and we all admire your good intentions. But we feel that people will be considerably more interested in attending if they have the opportunity to buy originals of your work. You understand, of course.'

It sounded like a statement, not a question.

'Of course,' I said, but my mouth was dry. I plucked a strand of hair from my head and rubbed it anxiously between my finger and my thumb until it twisted up into a small and wiry clump. It made a rustling and a crackling, like the sound of ripping Velcro.

'Great,' she said, 'That's settled, then.'

'That's settled, then,' is all I said. Because it really didn't feel that great.

The article was printed in the *Ham and High* on Friday and I read it off my laptop screen online. The headline read 'Carer with Cancer Creates a Lasting Legacy.' Beneath were four large images. The largest was of me, looking horribly well, surrounded by the older people at the Day Centre. Everyone was smiling except for Donna, who was frowning over someone's shoulder, her scowl like stone. Then there were two pages from the Life Guide: step-by-step instructions on how to change a light bulb, complete with tiny pencil drawings, and a page of illustrated life advice. I'd written things like 'Listening is a superpower,' and 'Saying sorry is a strength and not a weakness,' in a delicate and curling font, filling the spaces on the page with pencil drawings of the boys. The final image was another photograph taken following the interview. It showed Casey and Sue after having their heads shaved. Sue was grinning broadly, but Casey's eyes were large and dark, like an animal in danger. Her hair was puddled on the floor. Long, lifeless lengths that spooled across the lino.

I used my flattened hand to block the picture out and read around my fingers. The headline made my stomach turn. Now everybody knew about the fake cancer and the mention of a 'legacy' suggested that the cancer might be terminal.

But the remainder of the article filled me with pride. George Behrman had described me as brilliant and gifted. He'd written about me glowingly, not only as an artist but as a person too, and had included quotes from Frankie, Gill and Terrence, who claimed that I was 'wonderful', 'an angel sent in human form' and 'a reason to keep plodding on, who wasn't bad to look at'. I could imagine Terrence winking as he said that. At the bottom of the article was the link to the JustGiving page and details of the gallery show. I flushed with satisfaction.

The article had only been online for a few hours, and it was morning, so physical copies of the paper were still being sold in all the local shops – but it soon became clear that it had already had a huge impact. With trembling hands, I checked the JustGiving Page. The total had now reached over ten thousand pounds. Ten thousand actual pounds! It was hard to fully comprehend. But looking back, *all* of it is hard to comprehend: the things I said and didn't say. The truly awful things I did.

Ryan was asleep upstairs and Bo, Olly and James had gone to work. I had space and time – the thing that I'd been dreaming of since the boys were born. By this time next week, my life and family would have all returned to normal.

So, that morning I stayed at home and made myself endless rounds of tea, adding extra spoons of sugar. I even tried a facial mask from Bo's collection in the bathroom and spent the next few hours recumbent on the sofa, my face coated in collagen and detoxifying charcoal that promised to intensively hydrate and renew.

When I wasn't checking the JustGiving page, I watched TV, bingeing series that I'd never normally have a chance to see. The cat had sidled silently into the room and started sharpening its front claws on the side edge of the sofa. For once, I didn't try to stop it. Instead, I watched the fabric shred and violently fray, and I wondered what it felt like to just break something, destroy something.

The cat was probably hungry; I dragged myself up from the sofa. As I walked towards the kitchen it looped between my legs, wrapping its body around each ankle as I walked. James said this was a show of feline love, but he clearly didn't know the cat. As I stretched to reach the pet food, wedged into the awkward space between the cupboards and the ceiling, I almost tripped. I hissed annoyance at the cat, then squeezed the pungent meaty cubes from the small sachet. Immediately, the kitchen filled with the smell of boiled beef and school gravy. The stench caught inside my nostrils. I watched a thick globule of beige jelly seep slowly out and stick onto my finger, obscuring the pale moon of nail. My eyes watered and nostrils flared. I held my breath whilst the cat purred.

A photo on the fridge caught my attention as I went to throw away the empty sachet. Bo was nestled into Olly's chest. His hands had slipped towards the curving sweep of her backside. She had the sort of bottom that the boys described as 'thick', a word I was assured was now a compliment. The word seemed wrong, her bottom looking far from thick and more like two perfectly formed bubbles. I looked down at my own body, a body on the far extremes of motherhood, on the jagged cusp of menopause, with a bottom that was decidedly not bubble shaped or modern 'thick' but saggy, flat and disturbingly quite dimpled. No matter what I ate or didn't eat my body carried on spreading beyond the confines of the shape it used to know until I hardly recognised myself. It wasn't just my bottom that had changed over the years. My stomach slumped over the too-tight waistline of my underwear and hair was cropping up in places where it shouldn't really be. A soft feathering across my toes and hairs around each areola, which without the help of tweezers looked like tiny little Christmas wreaths. A furry celebration of humanity. My body was deeply disappointing, but I found comfort in the thought that it wouldn't really matter when I gained success. The world would judge me on my talents.

That afternoon was the pretend appointment at the hospital. I'd told my family that I was going there with Casey. James had tried to say he'd go with me instead, but I kept insisting that his irrational fear of hospitals was the last thing that I needed to be dealing with. I claimed that it was just too much for me to cope with given everything that I was dealing with and that the best thing he could do for me was stay away. He'd reluctantly agreed, but not before he'd asked me when I'd last seen Nel.

'She's teaching,' I had said lightly. 'I can't ask Nel to take time off work, especially this close to exams.'

'I get that. I just suppose that I'm a bit surprised. I mean, when your dad died, we could hardly get her out the house. She was always here. The woman practically moved in with us. But since your diagnosis I've not seen her.'

I shrugged. 'None of us will ever understand the inner workings of Nel's mind,' I said.

'It's still not right,' he'd answered back with feeling. 'I thought she was a better friend, or at least a better person.

But I guess you find out who your people are when things get tough. She's clearly not the woman that I thought she was.'

But then again, neither was I. I let him think that Nel was terrible, an awful friend, and I told him I was meeting Casey at the hospital when I was actually trying out a yoga class.

Yoga was something that I'd always hoped to do but I could never find the time for. The class that I'd seen advertised was in a church hall close to the North Circular. Inside, the hall was large and bright, flooded with light. I got there early and headed towards an empty mat beside the door. Women were arriving, holding bags with coloured mats and small foam blocks and fabric straps.

'Your first time here?' the woman who sat beside me asked. I averted my gaze from the wooden Jesus pinned up on the wall, his arms spread wide, his legs stretched long, in what appeared to be a yogic pose. 'You'll be just fine,' the woman said. 'Aria's so lovely.'

She nodded at a tall woman who was busy placing plastic candles all around the room. Aria's hair was thick with dark, tight, curls that hung around her face in coils. She wore layered tops in pastel shades that made me think of mountain mists and summer air and raspberries growing on tall canes, over a pair of yoga leggings. Her body was compact and tight, and her diamond-studded earrings glinted as she addressed the group, her hands clasped close in prayer across her sun-tanned chest.

'What a gift this sunny afternoon is!' Her voice dripped cash. Despite the carefully curated spiritual look her accent sounded like she lived somewhere like Kensington or Notting Hill. Aria began to walk around the room, spraying us with a citrus mist.

'Now let's begin,' she cooed, facing the room. Despite her obvious privilege it was hard not to be swept along by Aria's sense of joy and calm.

I'd never done yoga before. It was something other people did. Women who didn't look like me, women who had spare time and spare money. We started with a series of cat-cows and then progressed to gentle forward bends. To begin with, I was awkward and uncomfortable, arching my back, rolling my neck, breathing out on Aria's command with loud and elongated sighs. The weird movements and bovine noises reminded me of childbirth.

It was hard to maintain focus when Aria looked so un-believably elegant in her tight sportswear. I wondered how nothing more than stretching and relaxing made her thighs so small. It made no sense. And then there were the other women in the room, most of whom were tiny and made it look so easy. When Aria asked us to go into 'Downward Dog', the women quickly rearranged their bodies into triangles. I groaned and did my best to replicate the shape, awkwardly and without grace, my heels nowhere near the floor.

But after a while, I realised that no one else was watching me. The women were all focused on themselves. No one cared what I was doing or not doing. Occasionally, Aria would quietly come up to me and make a small adjustment, whilst still instructing the whole class. She would gently change the angle of my foot. Or press down on my lower back, to stretch my muscles a little deeper. Very soon I was enjoying the experience of focusing on my body in a positive way. As Aria guided the entire room through a final meditation, I realised that my mind had slowed for the first time in weeks. I breathed down deep into my belly and with every exhalation, I felt undeniably calmer.

Afterwards, when Aria was packing up the fake candles that she'd placed around the room with their battery-powered flickering flames, I went over to thank her. For a few moments during the yoga class, I hadn't thought about the lies I'd told, about my family or my friends or work, and I wanted more moments like that. Those rare fragments of quiet and calm. I wondered if I would have made the same decisions and acted in the way I did and told those truly dreadful lies if I'd only made the time over the years to focus on myself, if I'd only done some yoga. But looking back, I doubt yoga would have been enough to save me from myself. Because during the class, I hadn't thought about my family once or the monstrous lie that was playing out – that they all thought I was currently at the hospital.

Back at home, we agreed that we'd wait until everyone was gathered together for dinner before I shared the details of the day. That way, I wouldn't have to repeat any of my made-up news about my non-existent treatment for my manufactured breast cancer. We sat around the table with a frighteningly large salad and some sort of vegan curry that Bo had cooked. It looked a bit like wet cat food and apparently contained a lot of turmeric and ginger.

'The spices help with inflammation,' Bo assured me. 'They're good if you have cancer.'

I somehow managed to thank her, but all I really wanted was a beef burger with melted cheese, topped with a layer of crispy bacon.

As Bo ladled out the curry and Olly piled a generous heap of lettuce leaves onto my plate, I looked around the table. James was ploughing through a large glass of white wine at frightening speed, and Ryan looked exhausted. Not only that, but he also looked too bony. Ryan had always been quite slender, but now his shoulder blades were scalpel sharp. His body reminded me of a pencil that had recently been sharpened, and his cheekbones cut the kitchen air. My son was disappearing. I peered beneath the table and without his socks I could see his swollen ankle.

'Ryan!' I said. 'That needs some ice right now. And you have to see a doctor.'

'Mum, it's just a sprain. It's not like it could kill me. And I don't want to waste the doctor's time.'

'But you wouldn't be wasting anyone's time. Just look at it,' I pleaded.

'And anyway, I can't let any of my sponsors down. A few of them have already given me the money for the charities I've chosen.'

I briefly closed my eyes and rubbed my temples. I wanted the world to go away.

'Sarah,' James said.

I looked at him.

'Ryan is going to sort his ankle out. Please just tell us what the doctors said today? Is there a plan for treatment?'

James was fiddling with his wine glass, running his fingers round the circular rim, his hand constantly in motion. His face looked pained as he waited anxiously to hear what I would say.

'Well,' I began. They all looked at me expectantly. 'I'll have to have surgery at a future date, but for now I start with chemo. And the good news is I get to take it in tablet form, so I can stay at home, and it will have a lot less impact on our lives. I'm starting this . . .' I took the bottle from my handbag, the one I'd filled with vitamins, with its forged label, and flashed it briefly at my family. 'Isn't that great news?'

I forced a smile, but everyone else around the table remained silent. No one seemed to share my positivity. 'Well, I suppose that it's not great,' I said at last. 'It's still a chemo drug, I know. And the side effects are serious. All I'm saying is that things ...' I glanced around for one last, desperate time, '... could be much worse.'

On Saturday I woke up to a text from Sue. Apparently, her sister had agreed to see me free of charge for a private online consultation.

'That's so kind,' I wrote, obviously intending to ignore the generous offer, but Sue texted back immediately with her sister's email address.

'Send all your scans across to her. She said she can review your notes and images today,' she wrote.

I was staring at the message, wondering how on earth I should reply when Bo came in. She told me that Olly was asleep still, with another awful hangover. James had got up early to do the weekly grocery shop at the large Tesco beside the retail park. I presumed he was hungover, too.

Bo clambered up onto the bottom of the mattress, corkscrewed her slender legs and sat there looking frightfully sad.

'Do you want to go shopping?' Bo asked. 'With me, I mean.'

She was fussing with a strand of silky hair and looked so

lost and lonely that I felt compelled to go. Also, I needed the distraction. I didn't want to stay at home with just my thoughts for company.

Later that day, I found myself sitting across from Bo at a table in a café in Brent Cross, North London's shopping mall. On the table between us were two low-fat oat milk lattes – which smelled better than they tasted – and a slab of carrot cake for sharing, which Bo had mistakenly assumed was healthy because it contained a vegetable. I tried to ask about Olly, desperate to know if they were fighting still but she kept changing the subject. Instead, she carried on quizzing me about my future hospital appointments, saying that she'd come with me.

'That's really kind. But you have work,' I tried. 'And if Casey can't come with me then I'm happy going there alone.' My foot kept tapping under the table.

'Really?' she asked, attempting to catch my gaze. 'But why? I know if it was me, I would want some company. The thought of being all alone and going through this . . .'

I ripped a broken shard of nail from my little finger and stabbed the cake with fork prongs. The fork scraped hard against the factory-made ceramic plate and the noise sent shivers up my spine.

'I just don't think you should go alone,' she said again, shaking her head.

'Okay,' I finally said. 'It really doesn't bother me, but I

promise that I won't from this point on.' All I wanted was to stop her talking.

'Great,' she said, her brow clearing. 'So, when's your next appointment?'

I wracked my brain, trying to think of what to say to her. I picked a date.

'It's nothing big. Just a quick chat to find out how I'm feeling on the chemo. Casey has already offered to go with me,' I lied. 'But you can come to the appointment after that?'

I fixated on the cake, avoided her eye and wondered what new lies I'd have to tell to hide my giant, growing lie. I consoled myself with the knowledge that after the next pretend appointment I could tell people that the hospital had made a huge mistake. Bo would never have to come with me.

'Great,' she said. 'That's settled then. And this is yours,' she added, sounding pleased that I'd relented. 'You can have the rest. You deserve nice things, especially now. And carrots are really good for you.'

Bo smiled and put her fork aside, pushed the plate across the table. The cake was slathered in a layer of sweet frosting, obscenely thick, made with dollops of cream cheese and sugar. The surface looked like fallen snow, the kind we never see in London. I mashed it with the fork prongs. The cake was a gift I'd never asked for and most definitely didn't deserve. The sugar made my teeth ache.

I left it on the plate and sipped my cup of putrid coffee

whilst Bo reached into her bag and pulled out a ball of creamy wool and a clutch of crochet hooks.

'Do you want to do some crochet?'

'Thanks, but no,' I said. 'I'm fine.'

'No,' she said, 'You're really not,' which was surprisingly insightful. She fiddled with the gold hoop of her earring. 'You know that you should try this. I promise that it's brilliant for mental health. I've been following Tom Daley since the Tokyo Olympics, but I don't know how he knits like that. It's so much harder than it looks and everything I did just kept unravelling. So, I've started doing crochet.' She proudly showed me a small strip of tiny pale stitches, a rectangle a few inches wide.

'Are you making a small scarf?' I asked 'Isn't it a bit too warm for that right now?'

I tried to focus on the conversation, to not get caught up in my thoughts. Bo gently laughed and I remember that the laughter made her earrings swing.

'No, it's not a scarf. I'm making a blanket for the baby.'

My coffee sprayed across the table. How could my son? What had he done? Was this the reason they were fighting? Had this inspired Olly's drinking? They didn't even own a house, and they were both so young. So awfully young. Bo couldn't be a mother to a child. She was practically a child still herself. I had absolutely no idea how the pair of them could stop themselves from focusing on their own needs for long enough to look after goldfish or perhaps even a cactus, let alone a human baby.

'You're going to have a baby?' I wheezed.

Bo wiped up the coffee droplets with a folded paper napkin. 'I want to be a mum, like you,' she said.

My heart hurt in my chest. 'Oh, Bo,' I said.

The words felt sticky in my mouth and the lights seemed far too bright. I stared at Bo's small crochet strip, which she was adding to, wrapping a strand of milky wool around the fingers of her hand, and catching at the loops of yarn with the tiny metal hook to form another row.

'I taught myself by watching some tutorials on YouTube,' she said proudly. 'Did you know there's such a thing as crochet TikTok? I follow this one girl who makes crocheted bras whilst sitting in her car in random car parks. I think that her last video had something like eight million likes. I might move away from fitness and focus on my crochet. Or better still, combine the two.'

It was hard to comprehend that we were talking about TikTok.

'When are you due?' I asked, my eyes fixed on the beginnings of the creamy pale blanket.

'Sorry?' she asked, not looking up, her pristine face focusing intently as she formed another perfect stitch. 'Oh, damn. I've just lost count. Sorry. What was it that you asked again?'

'When are you due?' I practically spat out the words. I

felt like I might vomit. I could feel the bile swirling in the gnawing space beneath my ribs and the acid quickly rising, scratching in my narrowed throat.

'Oh, I'm not pregnant yet,' Bo said lightly, shaking her head.

The relief was overwhelming, until I realised that she'd just said 'yet'.

'Olly and I . . . well, we spoke about the cancer. We know how sad you are that your own mum never got to meet her grandchildren, and we didn't want the same for you. Just in case, well, just in case . . . you know . . .' Bo shifted in her seat. 'Anyway, we were going to wait for babies until we'd saved enough for our own place. But now . . . well . . . we thought that we'd get on with it.'

'Does that mean you've started trying?' I squeaked and reached a trembling hand towards the slab of sickly cake, trying to eat my feelings.

'Not really, no. Olly has been getting far too drunk lately to properly . . .' Bo stopped talking. She had probably seen the horror on my face.

'So, you're not pregnant yet?' I asked again for confirmation, as my mind spun.

'No, I don't think so.'

'Thank God,' I said, 'Thank God for that.' Too late, I realised that I'd said the words out loud.

~

The line of women waiting for the toilet was like the queue for female Portaloos at every festival I'd ever been to as a teenager. I took my place at the back and leaned against the wall, my bladder swollen and uncomfortable.

'Just go in there,' Bo said, steering me towards the one disabled cubicle, the one that doubled as a baby change, the one with no one waiting.

'Really?' I asked, chewing my lip.

'If you're not allowed to use it now, then when?' she said. 'Come on.'

She hurried me towards the front. The door was locked. We waited. I could feel the heavy weight of leaden stares from others waiting. A young woman finally pulled open the toilet door. She was wrestling with a pushchair, a new baby bundled in a car seat, shopping bags and changing bags looped over the padded handle-bar. The baby's face was tear-stained and the poor woman looked as if she had been crying too. I held the door open to help her.

'Thanks so much.' She briefly looked me up and down as I moved out of the way to let her pass. I smiled a warm and friendly smile, remembering the days when I was young and struggling just like her.

The woman stopped abruptly as if she'd only just seen me. 'Sorry,' she said shaking her head. 'But no. Just no.' She looked exhausted, shadows smudging the soft skin beneath her eyes, her clothes crumpled. She clicked her tongue. 'I never usually say something, but somebody really should.' She shook her head again, aggressively this time. 'People like you. You make me sick.'

I took a small step backwards and inhaled a sharp breath. The whole place stank of burgers from the restaurant nearby and the fake citrus smell of chemicals used for cleaning all the toilets.

'Sorry?' said Bo. I could almost feel her bristling as she barged past me, pushing her body in front of mine. A human shield of a friend. 'What did you say?' She glared defiantly at the other woman.

'She has no right.' The woman pointed at me. 'This toilet isn't meant for her. She doesn't have a baby and there's clearly nothing wrong with her.'

'Says who?' asked Bo.

'You only have to look at her,' the woman said. 'She's not disabled in the slightest.'

I swallowed hard, my cheeks on fire. On principle, I should have probably been offended. I mean, not every disability is clearly visible, and this woman didn't know me. So many things could mean I needed access to the cubicle, things this person couldn't know and wouldn't see.

'There's actually something very wrong,' said Bo.

She was standing with her feet apart, her hands planted on both her hips, and her voice had loudened to a shout.

I grabbed her sleeve, my cheeks burning. 'It's not worth it,' I whispered.

'It is,' she said, spinning around to face me. 'It's the principle. This judgemental, narrow-minded person shouldn't be allowed to make you having cancer any harder than it needs to be.' She turned back to the woman and glowered. 'That's right. She has breast cancer. You should be ashamed.'

The woman turned the colour of a Marzano tomato, which, according to his travel show from a few years ago, which I'd been streaming recently on the BBC, was a Stanley Tucci favourite. All the women in the queue just stared. A few of them were whispering behind raised hands. I could hear my heartbeat pulsing in my burning ears.

'I'm fine,' I said. 'I'm really fine.'

But I suppose that was the problem. There was nothing actually wrong with me.

On Sunday, I went to Nel's. I missed my friend. I missed our conversations, and I was desperate to make things better.

I was also trying to avoid James. The lying was exhausting, and even when my family and friends didn't ask me awkward questions, I could see the concern in their eyes. Deep wells of visible worry. Pigmented pools of pity.

When I left the house, Olly and Bo were locked inside their room and even with the door closed, I could hear their sharp, raised voices, which at least suggested they weren't busy making babies. Ryan was smoking in his bedroom. I remember the strong stink of weed and the seeping smoke which had filled the upstairs landing and was spooling down the stairs. I couldn't get away from the house fast enough.

Arriving at Nel's flat, I started feeling anxious, unsure of the reception I'd receive. Nel looked anxious when she saw me too, but at least she let me in and I pushed the front door closed behind me, leaving my flip-flops like I usually did beside Nel's shoes. There were her battered silver Birkenstocks, which were her favourite pair, some glittered jelly sandals and a pair of leather slippers that she'd brought home from a market in Morocco and that smelled distinctively of farmyards.

As I followed Nel along the narrow hall, my eye caught on a photograph of my family. In my memory I'd been miserable back then, working far too hard for not enough and unappreciated at home. Ryan had recently failed at school and Olly had just moved home again to live with us, bringing Bo with him, filling our house with too much noise and too much clutter. I was sure that life had been awful, that I'd needed everything to fundamentally change, but that smile and the laughter lines around my eyes suggested otherwise.

As I scrutinised the image of myself, I was struck by how alive I looked. There was a lightness to my body and something that I hadn't realised that I'd lost. I'd lied because I'd thought that I would gain something important. But in that moment, staring at the old version of myself, it was clear that I'd lost much, much more, that I was risking losing everything.

Including Nel.

Nel sat down on the sofa, crossed her legs and placed a cushion on her lap. She fiddled with a damp plait end. I could see the little girl that she once was, now the woman that I loved.

'God, it's been completely awful,' I blurted out. 'I can't tell you how exhausting the past few weeks have been. I'm just so tired, Nel.' I let the air out of my lungs, expecting Nel to sympathise, to say something.

Instead, she gave a single nod. Her silence left an empty space that I felt compelled to fill.

I rambled on. 'I had no idea how hard I'd find all this. I mean I'm hardly even sleeping. It's been insanely tough, you know.'

'They're new,' Nel said, not responding to my moaning. She was looking at my fingernails, neatly manicured and painted in the shocking shade of pink that Bo had chosen for the both of us.

'I've more time to spare right now. Bo thought I should try some self-care,' I said, forcing a smile. I looked down at the nails, bright and shiny. 'I actually made it to a nail salon. Can you imagine that?'

Nel bit her lip. 'Isn't that the shade of pink that's used to represent breast cancer?' she asked.

'Oh!' I said. 'I hadn't thought of that. Perhaps that's why Bo picked it.' I gave a shaky laugh.

Nel didn't join in, and my laughter petered out. I reached to rub the leaf of a large fig tree that was crammed into a terracotta pot behind the sofa. It felt like wax. Unreal. Pretend.

'Is everything okay?' I asked. 'With us I mean?' I so wanted it to be okay.

'Listen,' she said, heaving a sigh. 'We need to chat.'

I swallowed hard. In all the years I'd known Nel, I'd never seen her be this serious.

'I know,' I said, 'I know, okay. I plan to tell them in a few more days.'

Nel shook her head.

'Just four more days. The second that the gallery event is done on Tuesday, I'll figure out a way to tell my family that there's been a huge mistake. I'll put a stop to all the crazy fundraising, which – I don't know if you've seen lately – is going really, really, well. I mean, it's actually quite incredible. All that money that's been raised because of me ...'

I was rambling. Words were streaming, falling from my mouth.

'It's not just that!' Nel suddenly exploded. She pressed her palms against her thighs, clearly struggling to control herself.

'Really?' I asked. 'It isn't?'

'Well, yes. Partly,' she said, 'but there are other things.'

I shook my head. 'What is it, then?'

'It's just . . .'

'Just what?'

Nel picked up the nearest cushion. She fiddled with the metal zip.

'Sarah, you're not the only one whose life has changed in recent weeks.'

'What do you mean?'

'I'm trying to tell you something here. I've met someone.'

There was a pause as Nel uncrossed her legs and stretched them out in front of her. She pointed her toes towards the door.

'You've what?' I asked.

Nel flexed her feet. 'We've been dating for a month now.'

'Dating?' I asked. 'A month!' I said. 'But who?'

Then she told me all about the man she'd met online, some guy called Matt, and how things had quickly become serious.

I stared at Nel, deeply confused.

'Is this the guy who gave you that horrific STD?'

'I didn't have an STD. It was just a bad infection. Anyway, he has a daughter. She's called Chloe and she's twelve, almost thirteen. She's the most amazing kid I've ever met. This will sound insane, but I can see myself involved with raising her.'

'Sorry?' I said, not sure if I had heard her right. 'You don't like kids. You always say that teaching is a brilliant contraceptive and that you'd never have your own children. And anyway, you really hate monogamy!'

'I don't!' she said.

'You did,' I said.

'Well, I guess that people change.' Nel stared at me defiantly and I sensed that her words were actually meant for me.

'You've been so wrapped up, Sarah. In all the lies. In being sick. I've needed you and you've not been there.' Nel spoke softly. She lowered her gaze. 'Also, Matt has asked me to move in with him.'

'He has?' I asked. 'Well, if that's the case, then I really want to meet this mystery Matt who has changed your ways.'

Nel shook her head. 'You can't,' she said. 'Not now. Not yet.'

'Why not?' I asked.

Her hands were clasped together. 'His wife,' she said. 'She died, Sarah. She died almost three years ago.'

In the deafening silence of her pause, the realisation slowly hit me. I swallowed hard.

'From breast cancer?' I asked, dread spreading through my tightening, healthy chest.

Nel nodded. 'Yes. From breast cancer.'

~

By the time I left, Nel and I were in a better place. The awkwardness and tension had partially dispersed throughout the evening.

I'd made a serious effort to focus on my friend, asking questions that I should have asked her weeks before. I was genuinely interested in hearing about Matt. It transpired that he was a pharmacist from Camden, with a passion for road cycling and long country walks and cooking slow roasts at the weekends. He really liked house music from the nineties but hated jazz, his birthday and bananas. Nel said that he'd not dated since his wife had died, and the speed at which their relationship was moving had been a shock for both of them. But apparently, it 'just felt right'.

'I never thought I'd be a stepmother. Or any kind of mother for that matter,' she said. 'I'm worried that I won't be very good at it. I'm not the most maternal.'

I looked straight at my brilliant friend, with her plaited hair and her bright orange silky trousers. There was glitter in her eyeshadow and silver bangles on her wrist that jangled when she moved her arms. Gentle crow's feet fanned around her eyes and there were dimples in her soft cheeks from all the years that she'd spent smiling. Her fingers were streaked with smears of paint, from whatever she'd been working on at school. Small dashes of dark blue and flecks of green.

'You'll be perfect, Nel,' I said.

It was the truth. She would make a brilliant mother and all that I could really wish for her was that she wouldn't be like me.

For the rest of the evening, there were glimpses of the way things used to be between the two of us. Nel even talked about the gallery event, assuring me it would go well.

'Everyone will love your work. It's beautiful,' she said.

'And people finally get to see it thanks to you,' I said, gratefully.

Nel momentarily froze when I said that. She looked at me intently. 'What do you mean?' she asked, her eyes narrowed.

'Well, your encouragement and the gift of pencils and a sketch book . . . They led to all of this. Without you, I don't think that I would be here now, in this crazy situation.'

A shadow passed across her face.

My armpits pricked with sudden perspiration. 'I'm not saying that this is your fault. Of course it's not,' I stuttered. 'But if it hadn't been my birthday, and you hadn't given me that gift then . . .'

Nel stared at me, her mouth hanging wide open.

'Am I a total monster, Nel?' I asked.

She turned her face away without an answer, which was all the answer that I needed.

We were stood by her front door, surrounded by her potted plants that made the flat feel like a tropical vacation.

I slipped my flip-flops on and went to grab my bag, which was leaning against Nel's pile of colourful shoes.

'What's that?' she asked.

I followed the direction of her gaze. She was staring at my open handbag, which was gaping like a hungry baby's mouth. The jar of fake tablets was poking out, the prescription label facing up, the writing clearly visible.

'Nothing,' I said quickly.

Frowning, Nel bent and took the bottle from my bag, with the label that I'd drawn by hand. She shook it, scrutinising the writing on the label, the writing I was proud of. It was neat, precise and looked like print.

'What on earth is this?' she asked again, her face sagging with shock. 'Is this stuff real?'

I shook my head. 'It's not for long,' I tried to reassure her. 'I promise it won't be for long.'

'Oh God, Sarah,' she said slowly. 'This isn't right.'

'I know,' I said.

'It's sick,' she finally said. Her gaze rose up to meet mine and I had to stop myself from looking away. A new understanding seemed to fill her eyes. 'You're actually sick.'

The next evening James took me out for dinner. I tried to be excited. After all, this was one of the main reasons that I'd done all this — so that my husband would finally pay me some attention. But I wasn't looking forward to spending time alone with James. Now that he thought that I had cancer, he wasn't acting like himself. The worried look behind his eyes was haunting, but I couldn't find a reason to stay home that wouldn't make him worry even more. I tried to focus on the positives. Eating something that hadn't first been scrutinised by Bo for its anti-cancer properties was actually quite appealing and I needed to take my mind off Nel.

So, I found myself at Saffron Moon, sitting opposite my husband. Over a plate of butter chicken and lamb rogan josh, with a side serving of poppadoms and pilau rice topped with a dollop of raita, James made a big announcement.

'I'm quitting work,' he brightly said. He took a large swig from his cold bottle of Cobra and let out a sigh of satisfaction.

He waited for me to say something, clearly under the impression that I'd be pleased too, but I had no idea what I should say.

I put my wine glass down and blankly stared at him. 'You're doing what?' I finally asked.

'Well, I'm not quitting work entirely, but I'm taking a long stretch of unpaid leave. I've told all of my colleagues that I'm taking a sabbatical.'

'Oh God,' I said.

I rubbed my sweaty palms across my thighs, leaving hand-prints on my trousers. My skin felt damp and clammy, as if my fear had turned to liquid. A waiter headed over, and I gave a firm shake of my head. The man stopped in his tracks, then backed away.

'Your cancer … Well, it's made me re-evaluate my life. You're the thing that means the most to me. I want to spend all of my time with you.'

'But what about your income?' I desperately whined.

'We'll work it out. We'll just make do with less. Some things are more important.'

'But we might need it! We might need that money in the future.' I was thinking of the baby that Bo and Olly were planning to conceive and the flat that they might need help with. And Ryan who showed no signs of ever moving out. And the life that stretched ahead of us.

'We'll use the money in our savings,' James paused then said, 'And we can cut back on our spending. We'll be just fine. Being together is the most important thing right now, even if financially we'll have far less.'

James smiled and reached across the table. I didn't move. My hands stayed firmly on my thighs, sweaty and intractable.

'But …' I was panicking. Cancer was my only hope. It was the only thing that might get through to James.

'What if I can't work anymore? We won't have my income either. And I might need experimental treatment.' I said in desperation. 'I might need to fly to Germany. Or a clinic in America. There might be some drug trial abroad and those things – they all cost money, James. Your income, it could save my life.'

That quietened James. He looked thoughtful, then subdued.

'I'll speak to work tomorrow,' he finally agreed. 'I'll tell them I'm not leaving. To be honest, the whole team will probably be relieved. You're right, we should be sensible.'

The waiter kept on glancing over at our untouched plates from his position in the corner by the bar. Eventually James slunk off to the bathroom and the waiter ventured over looking nervous.

'Is everything okay, madam?'

'With the food or with my life right now?' I asked, rubbing my forehead. There was a pain in both my temples.

The poor man shifted from foot to foot.

'The food is great,' I finally said.

He glanced down at the pile of untouched food and at my unused cutlery. As he walked away, I downed my wine and closed my eyes. I remember feeling tired. So tired I could have slept right there, with my face down on the table, my cheek pressed flat against the tablecloth. I wanted more than anything for the lying to be over. And it very, very nearly was.

It was the Monday before the gallery show. I was supposed to be at work but decided that I couldn't face my colleagues or any of the older people being kind to me. Their sympathy was not deserved. I called in sick, not knowing that I wouldn't be attending work at the Day Centre ever again. Or any other Day Centre.

'Of course,' Sue said. 'We'll find a way to manage. We all understand.'

I felt sick inside when she said that. I told Sue that I desperately needed to rest. I think I even told her that the chemo drugs I'd started had made me feel really tired.

'The side effects are terrible,' I lied.

'Just before you go,' she said, 'my sister is still waiting. She said she hasn't got your scans. And time makes all the difference with these things.'

I promised Sue that I'd send them in the next few hours, although I obviously had no intention of contacting her sister and there were no scans to send her if I'd wanted to. I tried to keep myself distracted with even more TV, but I found I couldn't stand the sight of the brown sofa. My legs were feeling restless, my eyes were strained and my brain felt fried.

I kept checking the total of donations and instead of feeling satisfied I found myself praying that the number would just disappear, that everyone would take all of their money back and put an end to this whole nightmare. I was exhausted. When I'd eventually fallen asleep the night before I'd kept waking up, drenched through with sweat that for once was unrelated to my hormones. The dreams were vivid and frightening. Dark wolves with fangs and savage beasts, masked men threatening my family. I'd even had an awful nightmare that I'd found the cat crushed by a car, its back broken, its body stiff and its limbs bent at strange angles.

Now, I was hoovering the stairs carpet and feeling uncontrollably anxious. I couldn't shake the sickening fear that I'd monumentally messed things up in a way that was unfixable. What if I'd pushed the lie to a point that was beyond repair? I wanted desperately to speak to Nel about the fake chemo and to explain myself, but I didn't have the words. I would need to wait for one more day until the exhibition at the gallery and, after that, I could make things right. I *would* make things right. With Nel, with James, with everyone. In the meantime, I kept cleaning.

I was lugging the hoover up each individual step so that I could reach the dust deep in the crevices, when Bo called me.

'Don't panic,' was the first thing that she said.

I panicked instantly. My stomach churned, oily with fear, and I sank to sit down on the stairs.

'Everything's going to be okay,' she said. 'But Olly is in A&E.'

'He's where?' I squeaked.

'I don't know all the details yet. He was rambling when

he called me and then he hung up when a nurse arrived to triage him, but he's done something to his hand.'

'How bad is it?' I asked.

'Apparently there's a lot of blood. I'm already at the tube station but there's an issue with the train tracks. All the Northern Line trains have just been cancelled. Can you get to him?' Bo asked.

James and I took separate cabs as we hurried to our eldest son, and if I close my eyes, I can still remember how I felt as I ran into the building.

'My son,' I panted at reception. 'He's here somewhere.'

I gave the man behind the pane of safety glass Olly's name and date of birth.

'I'm all right, Mum. It's not that bad,' Olly said, the second that I saw him.

I'm obviously no doctor but from where I was it looked that bad. Olly's right hand was wrapped in bandages, and his shirt was stained a frightening red. Somebody kind had draped a cellular blue blanket round his shoulders, the shade a faded cobalt.

'Oh God, Olly!' James appeared beside me, having pulled the thin curtain back and squeezed himself into the space next to the bed. James's tie was at an angle, and his face was pale and drenched with sweat. I caught his eye, knowing just how much he hated hospitals. I could hear his ragged breathing.

'Please don't fuss. It's not that big a deal. I might just need some minor surgery,' Olly said.

'Surgery?' I said, my voice high-pitched. 'An operation on your hand? There's nothing minor about that! What happened, Olly?'

'Nothing,' he said, sounding childish and churlish, fiddling with the edges of the blue blanket. He rubbed the fabric with his finger and his thumb, repeatedly, religiously, and I was reminded of his toy rabbit whose cotton ears he'd rub when he was younger and still sucked his thumb. I stared at him. A mother's stare. He said nothing.

I pressed my face into my palms, pushing hard against my eye sockets. When I pulled my hands away it took a minute for my eyes to readjust to the bright lights. I wished that I could hide inside the darkness.

'Fine,' Olly said. 'This prospective client complained. He was insanely rude. A total dick. And my boss, she just believed the shitty things he said.'

'And?' I asked.

James was swaying slightly, clearly trying to keep his breathing calm.

'And, what?'

'What happened to your hand, Olly?' James said, snapping back into the present, tugging at his tie.

'I might have lost my temper. Just for a second. I . . . I punched a door and broke the glass.' Olly shifted in the bed.

I watched him wince and felt his pain jolt through me. Every mother's curse. 'I've also sort of lost my job,' he added.

James left briefly to get some air and I slumped into the plastic chair beside the bed. Olly closed his eyes and said nothing. When James returned, he was holding out some chocolate for our surly son, who was unappreciative it seemed, as well as unemployed. With no job, Olly and Bo could never afford to have a baby and would have to live with us forever, just like Ryan. I took the bar of Cadbury's chocolate out of James's hand, broke the corner off and ate it. 'He's nil-by-mouth,' I said by way of explanation. No one spoke about the sugar or the dairy.

After another scan, the specialist informed us there was no damage to the nerve endings and that Olly had been lucky, needing only superficial stitches. His hand would have to stay bandaged for a few weeks, after which he'd be referred for specialist physio. When I told Olly he was lucky, he just laughed.

'I feel really lucky, Mum. So very, very, lucky that my mum is sick and that I lost my job,' he said, his words slurring with exhaustion.

Eventually, we were allowed to take our son home with some painkillers and an extensive list of follow-up appointments with the physio team. James looked relieved that we were leaving. As we fought our way out of the crowded waiting room, past an old man with a black eye and a bleeding lip, and a woman with a sick bowl, I walked straight into him.

'It's Mrs Fernby, isn't it?' said a familiar voice.

I took a step backwards and saw that I was facing Dr Duggs. I remember being shocked by just how short he was, something that I hadn't realised when he'd been sitting at a desk. Moisture was gathered on his forehead, like raindrops on a bus window, and he dabbed his face with a compact wad of tissues that he pulled from out his pocket. The air began to feel thick, like Bisto gravy left unstirred. My armpits drenched, whilst my head pounded.

He frowned. 'Is everything okay?' he asked. 'You're not worried still? Is there something that you think we missed?'

'No, it's my eldest son,' I mumbled, trying to edge away. James was walking beside Olly just ahead of me and they'd almost made it through the large revolving doors. I focused on my husband's back, willing him to keep going, when my handbag slipped down from my shoulder to my elbow, glided past my wrist, finally falling through my fingers. It only took a moment. Then my handbag hit the floor. The contents spread across the ground. Paper and pens, a tiny blister pack of paracetamol that was missing half the tablets, a lip balm and a small booklet of bright red stamps that cost more than a train ticket to deliver all the post myself . . . and the brown bottle of fake chemo.

My heartbeat lurched.

My world stopped.

My organs spun inside me.

Dr Duggs crouched down to gather up my things and I reeled towards the bottle, aiming at it with my foot, kicking at it sharply. It skittered across the floor. My pulse thundered inside my ears, my blood an audible thrum. I was dizzy now and trembling as I crouched down too.

'Ahhh, I see,' he said.

Thank God he hadn't noticed the bottle.

'I hope it's nothing serious?' he said.

I needed him to stop talking and go away.

'He's going to be okay,' I said.

I glanced towards the bottle that had found a final resting place underneath a plastic chair, wedged against the skirting board.

I let out a stream of breath.

'Well, at least we gave you some good news,' he said.

I froze the moment that he said that.

'I don't always have the chance to tell my patients that there's nothing wrong. It's the best part of my job, you know!'

Dr Duggs smiled at me broadly and stretched an arm to grab an errant biro that was just in reach.

'Sarah?' James asked from somewhere above. I saw his shoes enter my eyeline, the scuffed leather stretched across his toes, the bottoms of his suit trousers. He had come back inside to find me. 'Is everything alright?' he asked.

Dr Duggs and I stood up. James glanced at the doctor's face and then at mine, a question furrowing his brow.

'Fine, it's fine,' I swiftly said, cramming the pen into my handbag.

I had no idea how long James had been standing there. I had no idea exactly what he'd heard. The blood drained from my limbs and it left my body reeling.

'It's fine,' I said again, forcing a smile.

'I'll see you all at home then,' James said after a while. 'I need to head back to the office to quickly finish up a couple of things.'

There was nothing in his voice that sounded strained or strange, and it seemed like such a normal thing for James to say. I smiled then. A genuine smile. The relief was over-whelming. As I turned back towards the doctor, James walked away into the crowd.

In the time that I'd been out, Ryan had washed his pillow covers and his duvet. They were hanging on the washing line, pegged between two scraggy trees. The sheets billowed and reminded me of a Kate Bush music video. Ryan was attacking the long grass with the lawnmower, an ancient flimsy plastic thing that he'd plugged in through the open kitchen window.

As a child Ryan had always been thin. He found meal-times a boring chore. His favourite thing for dinner was plain pasta tubes, but without sauce or any seasoning, not even butter or olive oil, and eaten with his fingers. I'd spend long hours with a hand blender, attempting to hide vegetables in everything and anything, including courgettes in a chocolate cake. But despite his strong dislike for foods, he'd never looked unwell before.

Now his ribs were showing in his back like piano keys and he was limping very badly still.

'Shit. What happened to your hand, Olly?' Ryan asked his brother, coming back inside. He gestured at the bandaged hand, his mouth open. I remember that he smelled of sweat and fresh, cut grass.

'Well, I lost my job but according to our mother, I got lucky. You should probably just ask her.' Olly spat the words out, sounding furious. At everything. But mainly me.

Ryan paused, unsure of what was happening or where the animosity had come from.

'Don't speak to Mum like that,' Ryan said slowly. 'Whatever you've done, it's not her fault.'

'Or what?' asked Olly angrily.

Ryan glowered at his brother then, his face becoming thunderous.

'I take it from your hand that you hit someone. Do you want to try your left hand too?'

Olly took a step towards his brother.

'Enough,' I said, slamming my hands down on the worktop.

Ryan breathed out slowly through his nose, clearly gathering some patience. 'Look, I'm sorry that you lost your job. But that's not my fault,' Ryan tried, his face creased in confusion.

'Well at least I had a job to lose.' Olly hissed the words at Ryan, before storming out.

We were left there, standing in the kitchen, my emaciated son and me.

James hardly spoke to us that evening. I assumed that he was angry with Olly, appalled that our son had lost his temper and his job. But James's silence was unusual and a part of me kept wondering if perhaps he'd overheard my conversation in the hospital with Dr Duggs. The worry spun around my head, but I dismissed it as ridiculous. I was sure James would have said something, said anything, confronted me. Of course he would. I knew my husband well enough to know how he'd behave if he had overheard. At least, I thought I did.

I forced myself to focus on the following day. The fact that people far and wide would shortly see my work was filling me with terror. A good terror. The kind of fear I felt when visiting the fairground that appeared each April in the park, the rides constructed overnight with what I always worried must be random screws, odd paperclips and some yellow, crispy strips of ancient Sellotape. The terror didn't stop me from enjoying all the rides and if anything, it made the whole experience even more intense.

I pushed my thoughts of James aside and focused on the fact that the gallery event was almost here. I let myself believe that the event would be a huge success and that the lying would be over soon.

When I finally went to bed later, I left James in the kitchen with his laptop, claiming that he had work to do. He sat at the table, staring at the screen, the blue light casting shadows on his tired face.

'Night, love,' I called from the stairs, but I'm not sure if he heard me.

In bed, I stretched my legs into the place James normally occupied. I shuddered as my feet were met with empty space. The sheets felt cold, the bed too large and empty without him lying there. The room felt deeply silent, too. There was a heaviness and a feeling that I couldn't place until I realised it was loneliness – the loneliness that comes from being isolated with a lie. I longed to hear my husband breathe, the sound that acted as a constant metronome, counting out the beats of all my married nights, our married life.

I found a book and tried to read but it was impossible to focus. I kept imagining all the people in the gallery. They would swarm like bees around my work, chatting avidly about my skills. People would comment that my talents had been wasted looking after everyone for all these years when I really should have been drawing. It was finally time for me to shine. I would be a real artist. A proper, working artist. Someone to be applauded. A professional. Even Nel, who sold her paintings to supplement her teaching wage, hadn't had the chance to show her work in a gallery as prominent as this. I had very nearly made it. Very nearly. I was so, so close. And then the lying would have been worth it.

I fell asleep alone that night imagining marvellous accolades, and when I woke, James wasn't there, just an indentation in the mattress. Before James thought that I was sick, he would often leave for work early. I assumed he'd got an early start so he could leave on time to make it to the gallery that evening. I assumed all wrong.

Swinging my legs out of the bed, I heard a familiar whining sound. The cat was mewling at the bottom of my bed, demanding my attention. I looked across and there it was. A pigeon's wing. A single wing, abandoned on the carpet. Perfectly intact, the feathers splayed flat and streaked with smears of blood. It was as if the feathers had been dipped in ink, and there was garnet red across the floor.

I screamed in fright.

The cat simply purred.

I could feel my heartbeat pulsing in my throat as I held my breath and tried to listen for the pigeon pair who lived together on our flaking window ledge. Nothing. Just an awful silence, an absence and an emptiness that was finally interrupted by my phone pinging.

I grabbed my phone, my hands shaking. Casey had sent a video she'd made the day before at work, of all the older people from the Day Centre, wishing me luck for the exhibition. I watched intently, my hand pressed to my pounding chest. Terrence's face filled the small screen as he beamed. He looked even scruffier than usual. His hair was like a kitchen mop that someone needed to replace, white tufts sprouting at angles, and his shirt was stained. My heart slowed when I saw his face but then the camera panned to Donna in her summer dress, a chiffon silk with a pattern of red roses. Red beads hung loose around her crinkled neck, and she wore a bright-red lipstick, but her face was grim. She didn't smile. I tried to reassure myself that everything was going to be okay. Just a few more hours. A few more lies. And then it would be over.

It was Tuesday and my time had come. The sketchbook had been carefully dissected, and each sketch had been encased in a made-to-measure walnut frame. I examined the bevelled edges of the double mounts, admired the non-reflective glass. Pinching the soft flesh of my forearm, I slowly walked around the room. I tried to take it in; the work I'd done, the success I'd finally achieved.

I stopped beside the illustration of a medium-sized roast

chicken, large enough to feed a medium-sized family or a single teenage boy. Dotted around the edges of the intricate sketch were tiny, detailed depictions of whole garlic bulbs, sharp lemon halves and fragrant feathered herbs alongside instructions written carefully in my curling font.

'Doesn't it look great?' a voice called out.

It was Casey's friend from drama school, the gallery technician, Kai. He stood beside a table, arranging champagne flutes into tight cluster. He took a step back, surveyed his work and frowned, then rearranged the glasses. 'Your work, I mean. Not these,' he said, and laughed.

I nodded, forced a smile. I worried that if I tried to speak, I might begin to cry. Just months before, I'd been working at a Day Centre for the elderly, and I hadn't drawn anything in years. Now, my work was filling a gallery, ready to be shown to the public. At home, my family would be getting dressed, waiting to come and join me for the preview. I knew they'd be so proud to have a mother who had done something, made something of herself. And I only had to wait another day to tell them the amazing news about my health. How pleased they'd be! With everything.

Excitement was effervescing in my stomach, like the bubbles caught inside the champagne bottles.

'All done,' said Kai, wiping the inside of a final flute with a dry cloth. 'I'm just going home to change.'

Kai was dressed in some unusual Nike collab trainers, and

his outfit was a cross between designer priest and modern goth. Everything he wore looked ridiculously expensive. The trousers were wide pantaloons in black linen, and his shirt was a large cotton smock. Around his neck were silver chains of varying weights and I wondered if he worried that his home was going to get burgled. I couldn't think why else someone would wear all of their jewellery at once.

'Great,' I said, although I had no idea why he needed to get changed. His outfit seemed so carefully curated. I glanced down at my Zara dress that I'd bought for the occasion, in a style that suddenly made me feel old and in a colour that did nothing for my skin tone. 'Is it okay if I wait here?'

'Sure,' said Kai, 'if you don't mind being on your own. I'll be back at five and Lia should also be arriving around then.'

I checked my watch, an ancient thing, my mother's watch that I didn't wear that often. It had a faded leather strap and a face with tiny roman numerals. I remember that the watch was digging in, making my forearm flesh bulge slightly out on either side, constricting me. I undid the strap to loosen it, and the watch slipped through my fingers. It landed face down on the floor and when I picked it up, a crack had splintered across the face, obscuring the hands. My thumb pressed against the surface of the glass and when I pulled my hand away, I could see there was a slender cut. A sliver in the flesh. I pressed it with my other hand and a drop of blood escaped. Instinctively, I sucked my thumb.

'Oh no. Are you okay?' said Kai. 'Hang on a sec!' He disappeared, his white shirt flapping out behind him. I couldn't help but be reminded of Princess Diana's wedding train, the fabric white and billowing as she walked between cathedral pews towards her fate, her dress a ghostly premonition in couture.

'I'm good,' I said, my words muffled, still sucking at the coppery tang of my bleeding thumb.

'Here,' Kai said, appearing again. He stripped the flimsy paper parts from the back part of a plaster that he'd found inside a First Aid box. I stood by the champagne table with my thumb outstretched whilst he applied the small beige plaster. I remember looking down and thinking that the glasses looked like honeycomb. 'All good?' he asked.

'All good,' I said. 'Just a little nervous.'

'You really have no need to be,' Kai said, 'your work is truly beautiful. Lia and I adore your style. And your story elevates the work. Tonight is going to be a huge success. Just wait and see.'

My cheeks flushed hot as the compliment seared through me and warmed my body from the inside. I gave a weak smile.

Once Kai had left, I walked around the empty room, surrounded by my sketches. They really did look beautiful. True works of art. I thought about opening a bottle of champagne just to calm my nerves and smooth the edge of my excitement, but I worried that I'd fail to look professional. I began to pace. I counted my steps, moved the champagne flutes a little to the right, decided they'd looked better where they were before and then moved the glasses back again. I glanced down at my watch, forgetting that I'd smashed the face, then reached into my bag to find my phone. It was 4.19 p.m. Forty-one more minutes before Kai returned and an hour or two before the others came, including my whole family. I couldn't wait to see their faces.

There was a tiny circle on the home screen, a bright red disc, like the stickers people place on artwork that has sold. It hung beside the phone icon, and when I looked closer, I saw that there were twelve missed calls. Nine from Nel and two from Bo and a recent call from Lia, who had left a message.

Bo was probably only ringing me to ask if she could wear some of my makeup, borrow earrings or a top that I'd forgotten that I even owned. Before phoning back, I decided to listen to the voice message. As I pressed the phone against my ear, I heard the now familiar rich tone of Lia's voice, the vowels as thick as cream and the consonants all curdling. But her voice had lost its usual friendly edge. Instead, she sounded formal and austere. My breath caught in my lungs as her words played out, sharp and unrelenting.

'Sarah,' she said. The way she said my name filled me with

a sense of dread. 'It's Lia here. I've tried to call. I didn't want to leave a message, but it seems I'm left with little choice.'

I pressed the pause button to stop her voice. I wanted to stop everything. To arrest time. Instinctively, I knew that when I pressed resume, she would say things that I didn't want to hear. The sense of dread sat dense inside my stomach.

I took a breath, pressed play and brought the phone back to my ear.

'I'm sure you'll understand that we can't represent you anymore. Not with the information that has come to light. We're deeply disappointed and I'm personally appalled. I just don't know how you ...'

I pulled the phone quickly away, not sure that I could listen to much more. It felt as if my flesh had turned to liquid and my insides were dissolving. My eyes refused to focus. I blinked and pressed my palms against my eyes. I pressed down hard to feel the weight and imagined heavy silver coins intended for the ferryman. The darkness pulsed and throbbed and swelled. I tried my hardest to refocus. The world stayed blurred. I dialled Nel. After all, she was my oldest friend.

'They know,' she said, the instant that she answered.

A dull, low groan escaped my mouth.

'Oh God,' I moaned. 'But how?' I asked, although I already knew the answer.

I thought that I might vomit then. I slumped against the gallery wall. My knees buckled and I slid down to the floor.

'James,' Nel said, confirming everything I feared.

Squeezing my calves, I pressed my head against my knee-caps and attempted to compress myself. All I wanted was to disappear. Or for time to unspool backwards.

'Did he overhear? The doctor? At the hospital? Is that how James found out?' I whispered.

'I'll tell you when I get to you. James is coming too but hopefully I should get there first.'

Nel hung up with reassurances that she wouldn't be much longer, and I remained exactly where I was, puddled on the polished concrete of the gallery floor. I couldn't think. My mind was filled with questions, swarming like bees. What could I say to James to make things right? How would the boys react? How could I ever make this better now?

Around me were the framed prints of my sketches. They loomed above me, taunting. All the lines appeared con-torted, the images strange and warped. I looked up at the giant shop front. The pane of glass reminded me of the one-way mirrors featured in police interrogation rooms that I'd seen in films and on TV. Outside the sky was dark and grey, the clouds the colour of cement and a wind whipped rubbish down the bustling street. People rushed past, and I imagined they were heading home to families they'd not lied to. I watched the scissor movement of their focused strides.

I was desperate for my husband's voice, desperate for his forgiveness. When I tried to call, it seemed my brain had scrambled, and I was shaking as I prodded at my phone's touch screen with clammy fingers. The phone rang and rang, but my husband didn't answer. I tried Olly and then Ryan, but they didn't answer either.

Giving up, I hurled the phone across the room and for once my aim was decent. The phone smashed a small illustration of a parcel being carefully wrapped. There were step-by-step instructions showing how to fold the edges into perfect points, how to use a pair of sharp scissors for creating ribbon curls and how to tie a pristine bow.

The glass fractured and the individual pieces turned opaque as they shattered to the ground like viscous rain. Shards of glass littered the floor, throwing light at random angles. A sound escaped my mouth. A guttural howl. My life was now in pieces.

'Sarah,' said a familiar voice.

Beside me, a pair of narrow ankles peeked out below a pair of silky trousers. Nel crouched down low beside me. I grasped her hands and cupped them in my own so that it looked like we were praying. Slowly, she pulled her hands away.

'Nel,' I said, looking up at her with bleary eyes.

She was wearing beaded earrings and she smelled strongly of perfume. Citrus, cloves and cedar wood.

'He knows, James knows,' I wailed. Loud.

'He does,' she said, her voice solemn. 'And if I were you, I wouldn't go online right now. Everybody knows, Sarah.'

I groaned again, pressed my forehead back into my knees, stared down into the darkness that I'd made, my body folded round to form a hollow cave.

'Oh God,' I moaned. 'What have I done?'

'It's over now. You'll be alright,' I heard her say, the words lacking the weight of truth.

'I shouldn't have lied to anyone. I know that, Nel. It's just that everything got better. I haven't felt this close to James in years. And Olly and Ryan have both been helping in the house. Ryan even started eating vegetables. And this . . . all this . . . I achieved this!'

I lifted my head and gestured at the walls of mounted sketches, all my artwork in expensive frames. Nel followed my gaze and surveyed the silent, empty room, looked to-wards the shattered glass splintered across the floor.

'Was it really all that much better?' she asked, her voice rising and falling.

'What do you mean?'

'Well, Ryan is a total mess. I mean, your son looks ill. I worry if the wind blows, he might snap in two. And Olly is so angry, he clearly wants to fight the world right now. And have you noticed the amount that James is drinking? I've just come from yours and the recycling bin looks like you throw a party every single night. It's just not right.'

I shook my head, let out another groan. 'Oh God,' I said, 'What have I done?'

'You lied,' Nel said.

'I know, I know. I've ruined everything, lost everyone.' I spiralled into torment. The guilt pressed tight against my throat.

'Well, I'm here now,' Nel said finally. 'Though God knows why.'

I squeezed her hand with fingers that were covered in thick strings of snot.

'Did he overhear the doctor? Is that how James found out the truth?'

'Yes,' Nel said. 'And then he phoned me a few hours ago and asked me to be straight with him. He was so distressed. I couldn't lie.'

Her words hit hard. Nel hadn't lied. She'd done the thing she knew was right and told the truth. She'd told the truth.

Outside the large square window was a man wearing a navy suit, with his shirt untucked and tie askew. He staggered, thumped a palm against the pane of glass, bent his body over from the waist. We startled at the thunderous noise and turned in time to see him vomit. He heaved and retched impressively, spewed his guts until the glass looked like a Jackson Pollock painting.

'Disgusting,' Nel said. She scrunched her face, turning

away. I didn't know if she was referring to the vomit-splattered window or to the awful things that I had done.

As soon as James arrived, she left. I remember that she hugged him and told him she was here for him and promised that she always, always would be. My eyes were sore and all the crying had made my voice hoarse.

'James,' I croaked.

He stood over me. My husband had been crying, too. Even through my swollen eyes I could see that James was broken. His shoulders had collapsed, as if his soul had cracked. His face was pale and tear-streaked, his eyes an angry red. It's a memory that still haunts me now. My husband and the hurt I'd caused.

'But why?' he asked. His voice cracked.

I pressed my face into my hands and shook my head. 'I'm so sorry,' I stammered.

'Just answer me,' he suddenly thundered, in a voice I didn't recognise. His hurt had turned to anger in an instant.

James reached over and picked the closest frame. It was an illustration of a shirt, just like the ones he usually wore to work. I'd written detailed instructions on how to fold it neatly, when packing for a holiday, starting with the sleeves folded behind the back, and ending with the shirt inside a suitcase. I'd included little diagrams with numbered steps, red arrows and small dotted lines. In the corner, I had drawn James. He was smiling in the picture, holding a cocktail in one hand, like the ones we'd drunk on holiday together, and the top few buttons of his shirt were left undone. The drawing was a favourite. As it smashed against the wall, I felt it in my solar plexus. The awful realisation that I'd never go on holiday with James again.

'You need to leave,' James said slowly.

Painfully, I staggered to my feet, a part of me relieved to be given an instruction.

'I don't mean here,' he coldly said. 'I mean the house. I'll give you a few hours, but then I want you gone.'

And then he left. James left me on the gallery floor. He left me there. And James left me.

The key turned in the lock. I twisted it, pushed at the door. A 'Congratulations!' banner had been tethered to the bannisters with string, the letters glitter-flecked and shimmering in dusty gold. Balloons in rainbow colours were tied together in tight clumps of forest green and Spanish blue, hanging from the light fittings.

I slumped down on the bottom step, forced my feet out of my sandals. I pressed my thumb into a blister that had risen on my little toe. The skin was smooth, and fluid filled, and the blister felt like bubble wrap. The cat walked past, ignoring me. I longed for it to curl itself onto my lap. I wanted to feel the comfort of its body, and its soothing, calm hypnotic purr, but it wandered off flicking its tail.

The house was hollow. Empty. Still. Devoid of all the people that I loved. I sat there in the gloom, the hall steeped in my memories. If I closed my eyes, I could see Ryan as a toddler in his favourite shorts, struggling to tie his shoelaces. Olly banished to the naughty step, singing loudly with his head tipped back, his heels banging on the wooden floor. And James arriving home with flowers on Mother's Day, his arms filled with a bouquet of pink hyacinths, the blooms a mass of coloured stars.

I'd got it wrong. So awfully wrong. My life's work wasn't drawings for a Life Guide. Nor was it a gallery displaying expensively framed sketches, or my illustrations being hung somewhere on strangers' walls. The most amazing thing that I'd created was my family. We certainly weren't perfect, but I adored the boys I'd birthed and raised and the husband who I'd shared the lion's portion of my life with. My legacy, they lived with me. At least they had back then. And I'd failed and failed to put them first.

Outside the sun was dying. A single piece of Sellotape came suddenly unstuck, pulling at a small patch of beige paintwork as it detached from the hallway wall. The 'Congratulations' banner collapsed until it was hanging by the final 's', the remainder of the letters twisting as they fell, and trailing towards the wooden floor. It sounded like a moth hitting a lightbulb. The softest clunk. A sickening thud of singeing wings.

I took a breath and followed the cat. There were pins and needles in my hands and my feet felt like a soda stream. I scrunched my toes, tried to rub the blood to make it move and then I walked into the kitchen, the heart of my home.

Inside the empty kitchen, a large bouquet of roses wrapped in tissue and clear cellophane was propped inside a water jug, and left out on the clean table. Below the blooms of crimson petals was a spread of cards in brightly coloured envelopes, all with 'Mum' or 'Sarah' written on the front, in handwriting that I recognised. I edged a nail into a gap and forced the gummed paper apart to rip open the card from James. It was a watercolour of a grinning cat, surrounded by confetti flecks and the words 'CON-CAT-ULATIONS!'

I barked a sad and desperate laugh, startling the cat. 'You've always been a star to me and both our boys,' James had written in his familiar scrawl.

The words felt like a stomach punch. I pulled one hand towards my heart, pressed the other hand firmly on top, as if trying to staunch a fatal bleed. An injury no one could see.

My heart pounded at frantic speed, as I ripped open the remaining cards:

*I love you mum.*

*We all love you.*

I sank into a chair and placed my head flat on the table,

felt the sparkling clean and bleached surface press up against the fused bones of my pounding skull. I closed my eyes.

'I love you too,' I said out loud to all of them. But there was no one there to hear me.

# EPILOGUE

## Two Years Later

I pinch the soft flesh of my forearm as I stand over the travel cot that I've placed beside my bed. Clemmie reminds me of an artichoke, with her succulent layers of firm, sweet, flesh. She is pale and podgy. Delicious and dense. She has Olly's grin and Bo's neat nose and if I squint, there are echoes of my ex-husband in the contour of her jaw.

For a moment, I feel the overwhelming urge to draw Clemmie. I imagine digging out some thick paper, finding an HB, 2B, dark 6B, gripping the pencil between my fingers and thumb. I can almost feel the pencil gliding, smooth, across the empty page, and hear the urgent scratch of graphite as the outline of my granddaughter is forever pressed onto the paper. For a split second, I wonder if I finally could. If I could bring myself to draw again.

My phone pings as I watch Clemmie clasping at her clutch of creamy blanket as she sleeps. The crocheted blanket that her mother made with love. I drag my phone out of my pocket. I fumble, trying to silence it, desperate not to disturb the sleeping baby. Bo and Olly will be here soon to pick her up and I want to hand a happy baby back. A baby who is fed and clean, not overtired and grisly. I want to make sure that my son will leave his daughter here the next time that he goes away. I want to prove that I'm a person to be trusted.

'Can you work a few more hours this week? We have friends coming for dinner Thursday night so the kitchen might need extra time.'

I sigh loudly reading the text. It's the house I hate to clean the most. I think about the woman with her fancy job and fancy clothes, who leaves her knickers on the carpet by the bed and slugs of toothpaste smeared across the sink. The things only a cleaner sees.

'Of course,' I type back tightly, wishing that I could say no. But the truth is that I have no choice. I need the job. I need to work.

Clemmie stirs in her cot. I watch her form a tiny fist, attempt to cram it in her pearl-pink mouth. A thin dribble of spittle runs down into the creases of her wrist as I put my phone away and bend to gently pick her up. She gurgles and I'm transported for a second by the sound. I swear that I can hear my boys. A reminder of the noises that they used to make themselves when they were only babies. Small, compressed notes of pure joy from a time when everything was good. A time before I ruined things.

We rock together by the window of the flat as I hum remembered nursery rhymes and we watch the people down below. There are youngsters hidden under hoods, a clutch of girls vaping, a couple walking arm in arm and a homeless man inside a doorway, his bedding smeared across the stoop.

A little further down the street, a group are wearing orange vests, all scrubbing slurs from the wall that runs behind the Job Centre. I scrunch my eyes, remembering those high-vis vests and the many hours that I spent wearing one, clearing litter from the scraps of local wasteland. I shudder, overcome by shame.

My phone vibrates inside my pocket and jolts me back into the present. I place Clemmie on the sofa as I answer it, wedge her carefully in the cosy space between two cushions and she grabs onto a tassel, tugs. I smile as I look at her, so grateful that I get to have her in my life – a gift that I will never take for granted. Especially after everything. After all the awful things I did.

'Are you almost here?' I ask, before he has a chance to speak to me.

'I'm sorry, Mum,' I hear him say. 'Our car won't start.'

I'm about to ask Olly if I should get the bus. I'm considering logistics, trying to work out how to get the pram along with Clemmie and her numerous things across the city on a Sunday night.

'Mum,' he says, then pauses, as if he's not sure how to say something. 'We have no choice. Dad is on his way to pick her up. He'll be there in an hour.'

Instantly, I forget to breathe.

When I think of James, I'm back in court, the last time that I saw him. The judge is sitting at the bench, and I can hear her as she calls me 'reprehensible'. Her words echo around my head. She talked about my disrespect for normal, honest people who were genuinely suffering. When the judge announced the sentencing, I remember watching James's face and it was clear that they both felt the same. I was a truly awful person.

Years have passed. But the missing is insufferable. I miss the young man that I dated and the husband that I came to know. I miss feeling annoyed by him. Oh God, I even miss his snoring. The gentle rumbling like a carriage on the underground. Or the beginnings of a rainstorm on a summer night. I think back to the months when we first fell in love, when I felt my heart swell in my chest and my veins pulsate with blood mixed through with shards of light from distant stars. Perhaps when James sees me again, he'll be reminded of those moments. He'll recall all of the love we shared and will finally forgive me.

Instinctively I go to dial Nel, to tell her that he's coming now, and then I put the phone away again, remembering she's asked for space. Not telling Nel my every thought isn't something that I'm used to. I shake the sadness from my limbs and pull my lips into a tight, wide smile, then head towards the bathroom, scooping Clemmie from the sofa on the way.

'Let's fix my face,' I brightly say, conjuring hope.

As I brush my teeth, each atom of my being buzzes, cells vibrating like a hive of disturbed bees. My clothes feel damp. My fingers shake. I bother with mascara and a light smudging of lipstick. I even find some perfume, dab a light splash on. Just a touch of scent behind each ear that makes me think of Nel again. Clemmie squeals on the bathmat as she pulls at both her tiny socks whilst I face myself inside the mirror. My hair looks wild and witch-like and I try to press it down with the flat of my palm, but that doesn't seem to help much. I wish that I had had it cut, the greys coloured. I wish I'd cared.

'It's going to be okay,' I tell Clemmie or tell myself.

When the doorbell rings my stomach folds. I open the flat door with Clemmie nestled tightly in my hip, and there he is. I cannot take my eyes off him. He's more handsome than I remember. A touch brighter. A shade more real. I stare, entranced, as if he were a magic trick, an illusion I can't quite believe.

'Sarah,' he says. And in my ears my name swells loud. It feels like home.

'Hello,' I say.

Such a little word. The greeting sounds like absolutely nothing when I need it to mean everything.

'How have you been?' James asks, looking at the carpet.

'Well,' I say, nodding with far too much enthusiasm. 'I'm doing well.'

I worry that I sound insane. We both know I'm not doing well. I really want to tell James that my life without him feels empty. I want to tell him that I dream at night that he's lying there beside me and that in my sleep, I wrap myself around his memory, tuck my feet like twine, our imagined limbs like trailing sweet peas. I want to tell him that the missing is so large that at times it feels unbearable. Instead, I turn to Clemmie, press the soft marshmallow of her nose. I try to smile and be grateful for the things I have.

'Do you have her stuff?' James quietly asks. 'I really need to go right now. The traffic will be building up.'

He doesn't move. He stands there in the doorway and then he rubs his thigh, presses the heal of his palm into the muscles just below one hip. His face contracts and I suddenly experience the overwhelming urge to soothe all of his pain away. To be his salve, his balm.

'James . . .' I start.

He glances up at Clemmie. At our perfect, beaming

grandchild. A human whose existence is directly linked to both of us. There is so much that I want to say. I know that we both sense it there; the weight of everything I feel and everything I hope he feels. The remorse and the emotion. It hangs there, monumental, huge, on the history of the love we shared.

'Please stop,' he says, shaking his head, but I know that I can't let him go.

I bite my lip whilst grasping Clemmie even tighter to my healthy chest. The baby clings to me like comfort. She gurgles, tugs my frazzled hair.

'Sarah,' he says, and he glances towards the window, as if the sky reflected there can offer answers in this moment. The corners of his mouth curl very slightly upwards. I swear I see the hint of a smile and I follow his gaze to see exactly what he's looking at. A pair of grimy pigeons on the windowsill. Their heads jerk as they peck each other's scruffy necks. They putter along the window ledge, and when I catch his eye again, I feel it there.

The possibility of something else.

A second chance, perhaps.

A second chance I may or maybe don't and won't ever deserve.

# A Note From the Author

To be human is to be touched by cancer. In the UK, one in two of us will be diagnosed with cancer at some point in our lifetimes. Every single one of us loves someone with cancer or has lost someone to cancer. Cancer is both cruel and everywhere. It's a diagnosis that nobody wants.

Which is why I was so horrified in 2020 when I read a newspaper article about a woman from Cheshire who falsely claimed that she'd been diagnosed with an incurable cancer. She let her friends raise money for her dream wedding and provided detailed updates on her condition, maintaining the lie, even when her own father was diagnosed with terminal cancer. I wondered what could lead someone to lie like that.

I dug a little deeper and as shocking as the story was, it transpired that other women were telling similar lies. Over the next few years more articles were published. In the UK, a woman from Kent pretended to have ovarian cancer.

In the USA, a lady in Iowa posted on social media about her 'battle' with pancreatic cancer and leukaemia.

The women seemed to have different motivations for lying. A few did it for the money, setting up GoFundMe pages or claiming government benefits. Others lied for the attention. One woman claimed that she was trying to get her family back together. She desperately wanted them to stop fighting and focus on her for once. Most of these women were normal women with no previous convictions and no history of mental illness. And yet they all felt that lying about having cancer would make their lives better.

And then there were the high-profile cases that shocked the world. Elisabeth Finch landed her dream job as a staff writer on *Grey's Anatomy* after writing a story for Elle magazine about being diagnosed with a rare bone cancer in 2012. The story went viral and Finch went on to become the authority on writing cancer-related plotlines for the show. Friends would even pick her up from appointments at the Mayo Clinic where she was claiming to have treatment. Elisabeth resigned from *Grey's Anatomy* in 2020 after her wife discovered her lie.

The *Scamanda* podcast, hosted by British journalist Charlie Webster, was the most popular podcast in the US in 2023. It followed the story of former school principal, wife, young mother and devout Christian, Amanda Riley. For almost a decade, Riley convinced her friends and family that she had cancer. She shaved her head and even falsified medical records. During this time people donated more than $100,000 towards her cancer treatment. Riley's lie was eventually discovered and she was sentenced to prison in May 2022.

In 2025 Netflix aired the mini-series *Apple Cider Vinegar*, a drama based on the true story of Australian wellness influencer Belle Gibson. Gibson was a blogger who claimed to have been diagnosed with an incurable brain cancer at the age of 20. She gained an online following in her quest to heal herself naturally with nutrition. On the back of this success, she launched a best-selling wellness and nutrition app followed by a cookbook full of recipes that she claimed had cured her. Gibson was described by *Elle Australia* in 2014 as 'the most inspiring woman you've met this year'. In 2015 Gibson finally admitted in an interview with *Women's Weekly* that she had never been diagnosed with cancer. It was all a lie.

These women all have different stories. They come from different countries and have different socio-economic backgrounds. They are a variety of ages. Some of the women are mothers and some are not. But they have all lied about having cancer. I kept wondering what could lead a person to tell such an appalling lie in the first instance, and what could compel them to stay loyal to that lie. And then there was the bigger question – would it ever be possible to empathise or sympathise with someone who could do such a terrible thing? Could any of us ever begin to understand? After all, it probably only started with the telling of one little lie . . .

Disclaimer: This author's note references publicly reported cases that inspired the fictional themes explored in this novel. All factual references are drawn from information already available in the public domain. The novel itself and its characters are entirely works of fiction. Any resemblance to actual persons, living or deceased, beyond those public reports, is purely coincidental.

# Reader Questions

1.  Did you empathise with Sarah at the very beginning of the novel? How did you feel about her initial decision to lie about needing a biopsy?

2.  Did your opinion of Sarah change as you read? If so, was there a particular moment when this happened?

3.  Do you believe that it is ever possible to empathise or sympathise with someone who has done such a terrible thing?

4.  What did you make of the shift of the family dynamics from Sarah first telling her family about her 'diagnosis' to those final moments before they learned the truth?

5.  Did you feel that Nel's character was a useful tool for the plot? If so, how?

6.  Did any other characters particularly stand out to you? If so, who and why?

7.  Sarah never refers to the family's cat by name. What did you think was the significance of this?

8.  Pigeons are regularly observed throughout *One Little Lie*. Why do you think this is?

9.  How did the author's writing style impact your reading experience?

10. How did you interpret the ending? Did you find it satisfying?

To discover more books from Charlotte Leonard, visit her at: https://charlotteleonard.com

# Thanks and Heartfelt Apologies

To my agent Jane.

Thank you for your incredible bad-ass professionalism and your endless patience. I am very lucky to have you by my side.

I am so sorry that this wasn't the uplifting love story that you were expecting.

To my original editor Clare.

Thank you for wanting to publish this book in the first place. What a journey we have been on!

I am so sorry that you're not here with me at the finish line.

To my new editor Charlotte.

Thank you for arriving with a smile and coffee and enthusiasm at the eleventh hour. You're amazing. I am so sorry for all of the last-minute changes.

To Aneesha, Phoebe and the rest of the brilliant team at Simon & Schuster. You're all wonderful.

Thank you, thank you, always.

To the Savvy Writer's Group.

Thank you from the bottom of my heart to every single one of you who gave me incredible advice and constant moral support. You have lived through the writing of this book with me, and I am forever grateful.

To Charlie.

Thank you for reassuring me that a woman who lies about something as awful as having cancer is a compelling idea for a story. Even whilst you were in the midst of having chemo. You are such a bright light.

I am so sorry that either of us know the word 'choloangiocarcinoma.'

To Kana and Ginny (my London Sisters), Rachel (my Bro), Debbie, Abbie, Olga and Michelle (my American Sisters) and of course, Lucy (my actual sister). Thank you for listening to me talk about this book for far too many years. To my mum and dad, thank you for being there for me always and for reading a first draft and for choosing not to disown me. I love you all very, very much.

To my sons.

Thank you for your patience, love and support, and for providing absolutely no inspiration whatsoever when I was writing this. You are my world.

I am so sorry that this book took so long to write and that I moaned about it so often.

To Nils.

Thank you for giving me the confidence to do controversial things and for convincing me that not everyone has to like a piece of work. Thank you for also agreeing with me that 'Sick' would have been an excellent alternative title! You make me brave. Thank you for everything. Always and forever.

I am so sorry you weren't allowed to design the cover.

I love you Nils Leonard.
More than pigeons.

**Charlotte Leonard** completed a law degree at Warwick before running away from Law School to travel the world. She returned to the UK and embarked on a career in advertising as a planner, where she fell in love with both writing and her husband. Her first novel, *Afterwards*, was shortlisted for the Bath Novel Award as an unpublished manuscript and was published by Simon & Schuster in 2022. *One Little Lie* is her second novel. Charlotte lives in London with her husband and sons. When she isn't writing, she is happiest swimming in wild and cold water.